PUFFIN BOOKS

## About Lucy Brandt

Lucy grew up in Derbyshire and now lives in sunny Brighton with her husband and two children. When she's not writing, she loves cajoling her family into walks across the Sussex countryside, or swimming in the sea.

Lucy also likes inventing new words and trying to sneak them into conversation. You'll need to listen out for that.

Follow Lucy on Twitter and Instagram @letlucyb #LeonoraBolt

# LUCY BRANDT

# LEONORA BOLT
## SECRET INVENTOR

ILLUSTRATED BY GLADYS JOSE

PUFFIN

PUFFIN BOOKS

UK | USA | Canada | Ireland | Australia
India | New Zealand | South Africa

Puffin Books is part of the Penguin Random House group of companies
whose addresses can be found at global.penguinrandomhouse.com.

www.penguin.co.uk
www.puffin.co.uk
www.ladybird.co.uk

First published 2022

001

Text design by Ken de Silva
Printed and bound in Great Britain by Clays Ltd, Elcograf S.p.A.

The authorized representative in the EEA is Penguin Random House Ireland,
Morrison Chambers, 32 Nassau Street, Dublin D02 YH68

A CIP catalogue record for this book is available from the British Library

ISBN: 978–0–241–43676–9

All correspondence to:
Puffin Books, Penguin Random House Children's
One Embassy Garden's, 8 Viaduct Gardens, London SW11 7BW

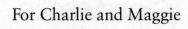

For Charlie and Maggie

# Contents

# 1
# Silly Little Mess

**FNIZZLE, THWOOOSH, KABLOOM!**

Leonora Bolt's hair was on fire again. And so were her eyebrows. 'Amazing,' she murmured, before realizing her head felt a bit hotter than usual. Grabbing a glass of water, she sloshed it right over herself. **SIZZLESIZZLE-FIIIZZZZZ!** Burnt brown curls stuck to her cheeks like seaweed. Great globs of grease dribbled down her grubby dungarees. And Leonora's dark eyes gleamed with triumph.

Now, to you and me it might look like she'd just taken a toaster to bits with a knife and fork. (DO NOT try this at home –

your parents will go completely bananas.) But Leonora was sure she was creating another awesome machine, a device to defy the laws of space and time, just like her last greatest invention. She'd call this one a **Removerator** and it would make horrible things disappear. Like wasps and cabbage and –

'Uncle Luther!' she cried, turning to find a shadowy figure looming over her. (She never could understand how he'd silently appear out of nowhere, just like chickenpox.) He was pale, razor-thin and extremely tall, which made it easy for him to look down his nose at people. His head was nearly bald, and his face was so sour that Leonora had actually seen it make lemons cry.

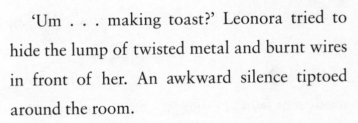

'Just what do you think you're doing *this* time?' he said.

'Um . . . making toast?' Leonora tried to hide the lump of twisted metal and burnt wires in front of her. An awkward silence tiptoed around the room.

'Why is my toaster in a thousand pieces?'

'I'm sorry, uncle. I was just making a new thingamy. It's designed to –'

'A thingamy? What's a thingamy?' he snapped. 'Is *this* what you've been wasting your time on?'

'I, um, just thought that –'

'You didn't *think* – you were too busy playing around!'

*Uh-oh*, thought Leonora, here comes the absolutely ginormous telling-off.

'I hate to tell you off! I only have your best interests at heart,' he said, with all the warmth of a man whose own heart had been swapped for a snowball. 'You need to work much harder if you're ever going to get anywhere!'

'I *do* work hard,' Leonora insisted. 'All day, I honestly do –'

'Really? When was the last time you used that pea brain of yours and invented something useful? Designed something intelligent, something worthwhile instead of this – this pile of *rubbish*?'

Leonora shrugged and stared at her toes. *The last thing I built was my best invention ever! He wouldn't call that one rubbish if he knew about it.*

'I – I guess it has potential. It could be useful?'

'No, it couldn't. It's totally hopeless. Just

look at it! And just look at you. You're a silly –
little – mess.' He spat the words out, jabbing a
bony finger in her face.

Leonora tried to follow his instructions
and look at herself. But it was tricky because
tears were starting to prickle at the corners
of her eyes. She would never, ever let him
see them.

'You're right, uncle, it's hopeless,' she
mumbled. Imagine his awestruck, spluttering
apologies if he knew about her finest work! But
she wasn't going to show him *that*. There was
another painfully long pause, then she asked,
'Are you going to the mainland today? Can
I come with you?'

He stopped circling the room and glared
at her with ice-cube eyes. 'Of course not!
I'm far too busy with my academic work.
A true innovator, a *genius* like myself, simply
cannot be distracted.'

'But I would love to see the mainland. Just *once*. I promise I won't get in the way or anything.'

'You? Come to work with me?' He started what could be described as 'laughing'. It was a wretched, metallic noise that sounded to Leonora like engine gears crunching together. She wished it would stop.

'Oh, how amusing,' he said at last. 'Perhaps if you weren't so idle and ridiculous, I could take you along – show you something of the outside world! Alas, it's not to be. You're not going *anywhere*.'

'But –'

'No buts. Get back to work. And tidy up this dreadful mess!' Before Leonora could protest, he'd spun around on his gangly legs and marched for the door.

Leonora sighed. She surveyed her chaotic room, which was large and round and topped with a great glass roof. Beside her, a metal workbench was buried beneath a landslide of tools and dismantled household appliances. Against the opposite wall stood a mahogany desk swamped with her sketches and drawings. And between them was a thin bed where her pet otter, Twitchy Nibbles, lay trembling on top of his velvet cushion.

'Hey, don't worry, Twitch,' she said, coaxing him out and stroking his rich, glossy fur. 'I've got a plan – a machine to get us to the mainland . . . *one day*. He won't be able to stop us!'

She gave him an affectionate nose-boop, then turned to the window to watch Uncle Luther striding along the beach far below. He was wearing his brown suit and tie and carrying a brown briefcase stuffed with yellow papers. He clambered into a speedboat and started the engine. It splut, splut, spluttered into life and away he sped.

She was left alone once more.

# 2
# Workshop of Wonders

Now, Leonora's bedroom/**totally-secret-laboratory/workshop** (KEEP OUT!) was at the top of an old, disused lighthouse. The lighthouse was on Crabby Island and Crabby Island was slap bang in the middle of absolutely flipping nowhere.

To the north – there was sea. To the east – there was sea. To the south – there was jungle. Sorry, not jungle, more sea. To the west – well, you get the picture. It was a tiny, forgotten sort of place. But it had been home to Leonora, Uncle Luther, their housekeeper, Mildred, and

Leonora's pet otter, Twitchy Nibbles, for almost all her nine years.

Leonora watched her uncle's boat finally disappear over the blank horizon. Her heart thudded in the silence. *Pea brain? Silly little mess? I'll show you*, she thought.

She snapped the window shut and checked the homemade cuckoo clock on her bedside table. It read 7.23 a.m. and five tweets precisely. Thanks to Uncle Luther's unexpected visit, the day already felt like it was bent out of shape. But he was gone. She had the next few hours, days – who knew how long before he'd come creeping back?

Warm morning sunshine flooded in, sparkling off bits of scrap metal, coiled wires, jars of silvery liquids, little mechanical gadgets and electric circuit boards strewn all around – making her workshop look like the most glorious treasure trove (or like a catastrophic explosion in a junkyard, depending on your point of view).

Leonora waded through the sea of cables to her desk and grabbed a bottle of special formula hair oil. She smoothed a few handfuls through her curls to repair some of the damage from her earlier experiment. Then she picked up a lump of chalk and began scribbling on the blackboard beside her:

- **FLAMEPROOF SHAMPOO**
- Musical socks
- Bee sting reverser
- Rocket pyjamas
- Magnetic cheese
- Original space/time disruptor

She paused, rubbed her forehead with her wrist. What to work on first today? Her brain often felt like a wonky Catherine wheel, ideas flying like sparks in all directions. And there was never enough time to build everything she wanted to. She also had chores to do – making her bed, washing-up, re-engineering the lighthouse generator to run off electric eels. Just normal, everyday stuff. Stuff that could maybe wait until later . . .

Leonora reviewed the last item on the board. She smiled to herself and pulled a key on a string from around her neck. Then she unlocked the top drawer of her desk. Inside was a box containing two contraptions. She took out the larger one. There it was: her most secret, most astonishing invention yet – the **Switcheroo**!

She carried this ingenious object to her workbench. Then she pulled on **ultra-magnifying spectacles** and set to work.

Inside the sleek metal case was a tiny but unbelievably powerful supercomputer. It could teleport a trillion, trillion, trillion (blinking loads of) molecules across time and space at the touch of a button. It could make objects swap places with one another! At least, that was the plan.

As Leonora tinkered with its microprocessors and single-handedly reinvented the laws of physics, she felt excitement bubbling inside her. She'd found a way to scan everyday items and turn them into data, then beam that data between two locations using *satellites* and *quantum computing*. Not so hopeless after all. One day she'd use it to leave the island and see the wide world beyond. That's why Uncle Luther could never, ever know about it. Leonora had to ensure it was a total, utter, cast-iron secret.

But secrets are slippery things that have a way of being discovered. Unbeknownst to Leonora, Uncle Luther already knew about her extraordinary machine. He'd been spying on her, and waiting for her to finish. And worse than that, he had plans for it. *Terrible* plans. The kind of plans that if Leonora had any inkling, she'd smash the **Switcheroo** to bits.

Just at that moment, a sound like weasels doing bad karaoke pierced the morning silence. It was Mildred calling her from far below. '**LEEEEOOOOO** – come and gets breakfast, me little sugarplum!'

Leonora's stomach growled. She carefully returned her Switcheroo to its hiding place. Then she lifted a snoozing Twitchy off his cushion, grabbed her rucksack and leaped headlong out of the nearest window.

# 3
# Crabby Island

Fortunately for Leonora, Twitchy (and the rest of this story) they landed in a wicker basket perched just outside the window. She yanked a rope and the basket lurched sideways like a seasick puppy. Then it plummeted downwards, stopping neatly 3.5 centimetres from the ground.

'Ta-dah!' she cried. Twitchy, on the other hand (or webbed paw), looked deeply unimpressed with her makeshift lift. He hopped out, let out a great **SQUARK** (cross between a squeak and a bark) of displeasure and scampered off towards the kitchen.

'Morning, sweetheart,' cooed Mildred. She broke off from pegging huge bloomers on a nearby washing line and bustled over. A great barrel of a woman, Mildred had a bulbous nose, an assortment of chins and blue eyes that bounced about in different directions. Her dirty apron flapped in the breeze like an enormous used hanky.

'I hope you're hungry,' she said, bending down to hug Leonora, 'because I've got Squid-a-Bix, roast pebbles and creamed cuttlefish in the oven.'

'Thanks, Millie, that all sounds . . . *nice*,' mumbled Leonora, gamely attempting enthusiasm. Mildred released her and smiled, revealing teeth like an exploded piano.

'Perfect. Could you bring in them fishing nets first? My old knees aren't up to it this morning. And I've gots a haddock trifle recipe I want to try.'

'No problem. I'll see if the winkle-pickers need oiling while I'm at it. Back in a tick.' With that, Leonora slung her rucksack over one shoulder, whistled for Twitchy and set off on her morning rounds.

Now, what Crabby Island lacked in size it made up for in wild beauty. It was Leonora's island – her own little universe – and she knew every inch of it. She could tell you where the peregrine falcons made their nests and where the wild iris grew. Hers were the heather-strewn headlands and the glittering, turquoise bays.

She knew the location of each rock, each rabbit warren, and all the very best sand dunes for face-planting.

Leonora had named the local hotspots after constellations, since reading the mind-boggling fact that all life on earth originated from the hearts of stars. (It's true – tell your teacher and get yourself a gold one.) Her first stop was Crux Cove, so she headed along the clifftops to the west, with Twitchy hopping alongside her.

Seagulls screeched in the warm summer sky. Far below she could glimpse the pristine white sands of Libra Beach, her absolute favourite place for playing games. Spin the Limpet, I Spy Seashells, Crab Grand Prix – all the childhood classics. She'd even painted faces on the rocks to make her games feel less . . . solo.

A little further along, they passed the crystal waters of Taurus Falls, where she'd first learned to swim with Twitchy. Then there were the rock pools of Lynx Lagoon. All sorts of bits of metal, glass bottles, old fishing tackle or driftwood would wash ashore for her to recycle into new inventions. She'd spend hours salvaging this beach treasure beneath wide, kaleidoscope skies.

But despite all her island's breath-taking beauty, Leonora's thoughts often skipped across the horizon to the world far beyond. Just where did her Uncle Luther go to? And why could she never go with him? Like 2+2=7, something just didn't add up.

She tried to imagine where he was, what he was doing, what the mainland was like. Was it true that children were banned from laughing? Was school really twenty-four hours a day? And could you actually be put in prison for eating sweeties? She had  no idea. She *did* know the mainland must be a bleak, gloomy place if her uncle liked spending so much time there. But she longed to see it for herself. One day.

At last they reached the **extra-fun-funicular railway** she'd built down the wooded gully into the cove. She was just about to step into the repurposed tea-crate passenger car, when Twitchy's magnificent whiskers started vibrating. Leonora shuddered. She knew they were tuned for trouble, like a seismograph detecting earthquakes. He stood on his hind legs and sniffed the salty air. Then a distant gargling sound invited itself into their ears without even asking.

### 'FNERGLE!!'

It didn't sound like anything she'd heard before.

### 'BLLAAAAARG!!'

It didn't sound human.

### 'FROOOOSH!!'

It didn't sound good.

Quickly, Leonora turned back towards Libra Beach and scanned the shoreline. Then – she saw him! There, on an inflatable lobster, she could see a boy. He was floating a hundred metres away from the beach, holding on to the lobster for dear life. But the waves were getting bigger and looked like they'd gobble him up.

Leonora blinked, rubbed her eyes. *Was she dreaming?* No – the boy was still there, still totally sinking. There wasn't a second to lose!

# 4
# Lobster Boy

Leonora raced back towards Libra Beach while Twitchy raced in the opposite direction. *Never bring a nervous otter to a rescue*, she thought. She tried to keep her eyes fixed on the boy. He was waving his arms for help, but the waves were waving the rest of him. Up and down and around he splashed, as if trapped inside an enormous, angry washing machine.

As she ran, Leonora scrabbled in her rucksack for something – *anything* – to help rescue him. **Seaweed armbands**, **a clockwork jet-ski**, **high-vis flotation pants**. Would any of those work? No time to think. She reached the cliff edge, leaned over and grabbed a zip wire bolted on to the rock. **'DON'T WORRY, I'LL RESCUE YOOOUUU!'**

she cried, pushing herself away from the cliff edge. For a moment, she just dangled in space fifty metres up. Then the pulley clicked and she hurtled downwards, feeling a rush of freedom as she swooped through the air like a bird. Her landing, however, was less swoopy and bird-like. She finished bottom-up, face-down in a sand dune.

Leonora staggered to her feet and spat out big mouthfuls of beach. But when she looked up towards the shore the boy was nowhere to be seen. She'd been too slow! He was lost! All was lost!

'That what you call a rescue?' came a voice from behind some nearby rocks. Leonora bounded over and came face to face with the castaway.

For a few minutes she just stood there, catching her breath and gawping at the boy. He was wearing a 'Snorebury Flyers' football shirt. His blonde hair was sticking up like surprised hay. In one hand he held the deflated lobster and in the other he clutched a soggy paper bag full of something.

Leonora had never seen another real-life, actual, human boy-person before. She felt a rush of giddiness and curiosity. Everything about him was different, from his glinty green eyes to his knobbly knees.

She reached forward and prodded him. Her mind wasn't dreaming up imaginary friends this time. He was *real*.

'Um . . . hi,' she mumbled. Then without another word, she pulled a tape measure from her pocket and started measuring his legs.

'Hey, what the – what do you think you're *doing*?'

'Hmmm?' Leonora briskly looped the tape round his waist.

'I said, what the – what are you *doing*?' The boy was blinking frantically as if trying to wake up from one of those weird cheese dreams.

Leonora didn't respond. She pulled a pencil from her hair and snapped open a pocket notebook. 'Height – a bit taller than me at 135 centimetres. Circumference . . . let's call it 56 centimetres.' She glanced from the boy to her notebook and back again. Then said –

'Weight?'

'W–wait? For what?'

'No, I mean, how much do you *weigh*?'

'I've no idea,' said the boy, looking more baffled than ever.

'OK, let's say 30 kilograms. Now, how long were you drifting out there?'

'Um, I dunno. Maybe a day and a night. Where *am* I?'

Leonora carried on mumbling, then finally looked up and cried – 'I've got it! With the prevailing winds and estimated time you were in the water, I calculate the mainland is much closer than I thought. Around 70.35 kilometres away!' She flung her notepad skywards and did a little happy dance.

'Oh, good . . . *great*,' said the boy. 'Please can we call my mum now? I should have been home hours ago.' Leonora paused and stopped dancing. She noticed his blue lips and shivering limbs. She calculated a 95 per cent chance of hypothermia unless she raised his core temperature by one degree in the next three minutes –

'I'm Leonora,' she said, scrabbling inside her rucksack for something to warm him up. She pulled out a seaweed arm band and ripped it apart, using it like a towel to dry him off.

'There – better already,' she said.

'Yeah, thanks . . . I think. I'm Jack. What is this place?'

'This is Crabby Island. My island. You're a bit, well, *completely* lost but that's OK. I'm sure we'll get you . . . home.' The word drifted away on the breeze, but Jack looked instantly more relaxed. 'Oh, great. Once we've called my mum, can we eat something? I'm so hungry.'

'Sure, we've got loads of food. And some of it's nearly edible,' she said. 'Come on – come with me.'

Jack nodded and followed Leonora. Up a

zigzag path they climbed, with the sun blazing and fluffy clouds doing backflips across the sky. If you absolutely *had* to be swept perilously far out to sea, it was a lovely day for it.

'How'd you end up so far from home?' Leonora said, as they reached the top of the path.

'Dunno. I was at the beach swimming with Jonny and Joel, my idiot brothers. They got bored and went to buy chocolate biscuits and I . . . I got a bit carried away.'

'I see.' Leonora raised a scorched eyebrow. 'And chocolate biscuits? What are those?'

'Um, they're biscuits. With chocolate on.'

'Oh yes, right.' Another pause. 'What's chocolate?'

'You don't know what *chocolate* is?'

'I know what it is . . . in *theory*. Just never tasted any. And I thought children weren't allowed it? It's against the law.'

'Whoa,' said Jack, a blizzard of question marks drifting between them. 'Where did you say we are again?'

'Crabby Island. We're a long way away from . . . *things*. Don't worry though, people get washed up on these beaches all the time.'

'Really?'

'Actually no. Never. You're the first one.'

'Then how will I get back home? My mum, dad – everyone will be worried!'

'Let's not think about that now,' she said. 'There's only a 76 per cent probability you'll have to live here forever.'

'Oh right, you're joking,' said Jack, flashing his lopsided smile. She smiled back, uncertain why this information was amusing. She'd spent years trying to escape from Crabby Island. And he wouldn't be laughing if Uncle Luther found him here.

Neither of them would.

# 5
# Round-the-Island Tour

Leonora calculated it was probably safe to give Jack a tour. That's because Crabby Island was smaller than an ant's tiddly-winks, so it wouldn't take long. A fresh breeze galloped off the sea and cooled their cheeks as they walked. Leonora kept one eye on the horizon, and gabbled like an excitable tour guide –

'So that beach over there – that's where I learned to surf. Got this old ironing board, covered it with candle wax and it really cuts through the waves!'

'You're kidding,' said Jack, as they watched the ocean smash the shore.

'And I built my first **death slide** on those cliffs on my fifth, no, my *sixth* birthday.'

'A death slide . . . aged *six*?'

Jack's eyes were like saucers. After a long pause he asked, 'What about all the other people? Where are they?'

'There aren't any. It's just me, Millie and my otter, Twitchy. And Captain Spang the ferryman turns up once in a while . . .'

'There's a ferry? Oh, phew, that's great.'

Leonora winced. 'There is . . . but it's not what you'd call *reliable*. Nearly sank on a couple of trips.'

'Oh . . . and there's really no one else around?'

'There's my Uncle Luther. He comes and goes . . . it's best he doesn't see you.' Leonora felt all the hairs on her neck prickle. 'Come on, let's keep going.'

33

Jack frowned but followed Leonora further along the sun-dappled headland until they came to three signs hammered into the ground. The signs had arrows pointing to forbidding black caves on the beach far below. They read:

ABANDON HOPE ALL YE WHO ENTER HERE – CAVE OF TREMENDOUSLY TERRIBLE TERROR!

DON'T SAY WE DIDN'T WARN YOU – CAVE OF HORRIFYINGLY HIDEOUS HORROR!

OK, GO ON IF YOU MUST – CAVE OF MILD MISFORTUNE!

'Whoa, what's inside those caves?' said Jack.

'They're the only bit of my island that's off limits,' Leonora whispered. 'Something terrible lives there – **THE FEARSOME FRARK!**

'The fearsome what?'

35

'The Frark. It's the ancient legend of Old Crabby Island. My uncle used to tell me the story every night. It's a sea lizard with twenty heads and four hundred eyes that eats people for breakfast. Mostly children.'

'Yeah, not the most relaxing bedtime story. You don't think it's true?'

'No – no, course not. There's no Frark mentioned in any of my books. Still can't get down there though. The caves are cut off by those cliffs. And they're also really . . . *pongy*.'

Leonora remembered all the times she'd tried to investigate the caves, and the many brilliant inventions she'd designed to combat the unholy stench. **Odour controller**

**bombs**, **de-scented candles**, **Pong 'n' Go cave freshener spray**. All of them had failed.

'I could help you, if you like. Can't smell worse than my dad's football socks.'

Leonora grinned at Jack. She wondered how bad football socks could smell. Did they also require specialist breathing apparatus? But before she could ask him this, and a squillion other questions about life, the mainland and everything, she heard Mildred calling from the lighthouse.

'Come and gets lunch, me little treacle pudding!' Mildred was waving her arms as if helping to land an invisible plane. Jack looked excited by the mention of pudding and off he set, with Leonora close behind.

'All right, me lovelies, and what's this, eh? You got yerself a playmate from school?' Mildred asked as they approached.

'Er, I don't go to school. There is no school,' Leonora reminded her.

'Course you don't, silly me.' Mildred chuckled. She leaned over Jack, her huge bulk casting him into shadow. Then, without warning, she gently tapped his head with her knuckles as if cracking a boiled egg. Jack fell backwards.

'Oh, look, he's so funny! I think we'll keeps him!' she cried.

'Millie, don't scare our . . . *guest*,' Leonora said, struggling for the right word.

'Course not, just my little joke. Well don't just sit there.' She turned to go inside.

Jack looked like he might sprint back into the sea. But Leonora helped him up, gave him a supportive punch on the arm and together they followed Mildred into the lighthouse.

'Keeps up!' Mildred trilled, as she led them into a corridor. Then along a corridor, through another little corridor, past a much smaller corridor and finally, into a corridor. Just after that they entered what can only be described as **THE WORLD'S MOST COMPLETELY AND UTTERLY AWFUL KITCHEN OF TERROR!** (Or TWMCAUAKOT for short.)

# MENU À LA MILDRED

* ———— 🌙 ———— *

## 🐚 STARTERS 🐚

Jellyfish Fritters with Squid Slime

Brown Barnacle Broth

Toasted Octopus Offal

## 🐚 MAIN COURSE 🐚

Whelk Melt

Boiled Black Kelp and Cockle Wotnots

Curried Sardines in a Gravy of Tears

## 🌀 PUDDING 🌀

Sludge Brownies, Mouldy Mussel

Meringue, Crab Pavlova

## DRINKS

Fizzy Fish Shake, Sand Smoothies or

Prawn Cordial

Chef's Special – see the board.

'You're in luck, I've gots a new menu,' said Mildred, cheerfully pushing a greasy piece of paper into Jack's hand.

'Maybe I'll have the Chef's Special, please –'

'No, he won't,' Leonora interrupted, noticing Jack's shocked expression. 'Thanks, Millie, but we'll have peanut butter sandwiches and two glasses of milk. Not fish milk. Or whatever the brown milk was that time . . .'

Mildred winked and began manhandling loaves as they sat down.

'Don't worry, I only eat peanut butter sandwiches. And the other food won't kill you,' whispered Leonora. 'Except her dried clam porridge – technically that *could* kill you. And the oysters in pilchard chutney. They make you *wish* you were dead.'

'There really nothing else to eat?'

Leonora shrugged. Making sure Mildred wasn't looking, she produced a silver device

41

from her pocket. 'This is a **Gruesometer**. It tests the taste-to-danger ratio and overall grimosity of foods.' The dial read:

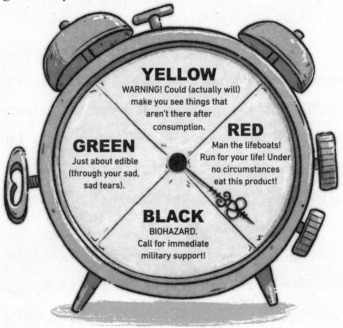

YELLOW
WARNING! Could (actually will) make you see things that aren't there after consumption.

RED
Man the lifeboats! Run for your life! Under no circumstances eat this product!

GREEN
Just about edible (through your sad, sad tears).

BLACK
BIOHAZARD. Call for immediate military support!

'D'you know what? I reckon we try these instead,' Jack said, producing the paper bag from his pocket. Inside were jelly babies.

'Some kind of . . . *adhesive?*' Leonora examined the sweets.

'No – you *eat* them.'

'Oh, right.' Leonora cautiously tasted one. 'These are – they're just – amazing!' she cried. 'Where did you get them? I thought sweets were . . . *illegal*.'

'Illegal? No, Mum buys them from the shop if we've been good.'

'Oh. If I've been good, I get to do non-commutative algebraic geometry. Same if I'm not good.' Jack blinked. He handed her the bag.

'How long have you lived like this?' he said.

'Lived like what?'

'I mean *here*. On your own.'

'Um . . . nearly my whole life.'

'Oh. I've always lived in a village called Snorebury. I've got ten annoying brothers and sisters. Jim, Jessica, Juliet, Jonny, Joseph, Joel, Jasmine, Josie, Jake and Dennis.'

'Blimey.'

'And a hamster called Hammy, a fish called Fishy and a sticky insect called –'

'Sticky?'

'No, Bernard.'

'I see.' Leonora wondered what it would be like to live in a village, with siblings and a hamster. It all sounded wildly exciting.

'This is all I've known,' she said at last. 'I don't have a big family. I'm . . . an orphan.'

'Oh, I'm so sorry,' said Jack, his eyes brimming with sympathy.

Leonora shrugged. She avoided his gaze. 'It's OK. My parents were lost on a sailing trip when I was three. That's when I was adopted by my uncle and we came to live here. But it's *my* island – I love it here. And I get to do whatever I want! Well, *sometimes*.'

At that moment, Twitchy skulked into the kitchen. Covered in white feathers, he was muttering rude words like **SQUEEEEEECHIN** and **NEEEEEAAAP**. (Luckily, no one could translate them until Leonora's **otter-to-**

**human converterphone** was finished.)

'Oh, not again,' she sighed, scooping him on to her lap. 'Third time this week those hooligan gulls have attacked. Thought my **anti-gullible spray** might stop them.' Twitchy squeaked what sounded like 'nope, it really doesn't.' Then he surveyed Jack through unblinking brown eyes.

'Hey there, little fella . . . so you've got your own island, your own otter AND you don't have to go to school?'

'Yeah . . . I don't have time for school. I'm too busy making things.' She took a deep breath. 'I'm – I'm going to be a brilliant inventor one day!' she announced. This was the first time she'd said this out loud to anyone other than Millie.

'An inventor? Oh cool. What do you invent?'

'All sorts of stuff – come on, I'll show you.' With that, Leonora jumped up with Twitchy and headed for the door.

# 6

# Mystery Celebrity

Jack chased after Leonora and Twitchy through the dark maze of corridors. Then up the spiral stairs they ran, giggling like dolphins on holiday.

The lighthouse had nine floors and Leonora counted them like the rings of a tree, one floor for each year of her life. The trouble was there was no ring for next year. Would she still be living here when she was ten, eleven – when she was twenty? The future, *her future*, was a subject that Uncle Luther pretended didn't exist. Just like Christmas.

Upwards they climbed, finally reaching a rickety wooden ladder and emerging through a hatch and into the workshop.

'Oh wow, did you *make* all this stuff?' asked Jack. His eyes darted about the room at a **mechanical spaniel** yapping under the bed, an **electric octopus** sorting socks, a team of tiny **brass monkeys** cleaning the windows.

Leonora grinned. 'Of course! I love designing animals, making them move with wind-up gears or electrics or whatever . . . plus they sort of keep me company,' she said, feeling her cheeks flush. Twitchy harrumphed from the corner.

'I've only ever made a rocket for my school science project. And my hamster weed on it, so it didn't even fly. What else can you make?'

'Those are my latest ideas,' she said, nodding at the blackboard.

'**Underwater umbrellas? A tickle-proof vest? Invisible space gravy?**'

Jack frowned, then burst out laughing. 'They're not inventions – they're way too silly!'

Leonora flinched. *Was everything she made silly?* 'Yes, all right, forget those,' she said, quickly. 'Can you keep a secret?'

'A secret? Absolutely.'

'OK. I've nearly finished my best invention *ever*.' Leonora unlocked her desk drawer and retrieved the hidden machine. 'It's a **Switcheroo**!'

'A Switcherwhat?'

'Switcheroo. It's highly . . . *experimental*.' 'Looks like my mum's hairdryer. What does it do?'

'It swaps objects around – teleports them!'

'No way,' said Jack. 'That's impossible!'

'Nothing's impossible if you use your imagination. I tinkered with particle physics and supercomputers and . . . ta-dah! This could transform our knowledge of space and time – even change the course of human existence!' Leonora's eyes shone like lightbulbs. Having Jack to confide in made her escape plan suddenly feel real.

'Whoa, cool,' he said, wearing the glassy expression of someone whose mind was being blown. 'You've got to show me!'

'Sorry, it's not ready yet.'

'Oh . . . and what are all those?' He nodded at a haystack of yellow papers.

'Drawings, designs . . . my uncle says they're hopeless, but I'll show him.' *Silly little mess.* The words kept jabbing her like needles.

'This is your uncle?' Jack had picked up a photograph.

50

'Yep, that's him.'

'I know his face. He looks *familiar* . . .'

'Hmm, I doubt it, unless you hang out with musty old professors?'

'No, that's it – Luther Brightspark! Whoa, why didn't you tell me you've got a celebrity uncle?'

Leonora narrowed her eyes at Jack. Then it was her turn to start laughing. Laughing turned into cackling. Cackling became full-on guffawing.

'A celebrity? My uncle? Good one!'

'Couldn't get me an autograph, could you?'

'No, I really couldn't.'

Jack looked confused, glanced back at the photo. 'Oh . . . he doesn't look like this on his

TV ads either – the ones with everyone surfing.'

The mention of surfing set Leonora right off again. She closed her eyes, savouring the image of her uncle on a surfboard. Brown tie slapping about his face in the breeze. It would pretty much break the dial on the **Stupid-O-Graph** she was building.

'My uncle's a genius professor, not a surfer. And we don't have a TV. He says they turn your brain into custard.'

'Oh, really?' said Jack. 'Because I like his Wondersurfer best. Every kid in school has one of those.'

'How – how do you know about my Wondersurfer?' The amusement drained from her face.

'They're in all the shops. And everyone has one of these too!' Jack picked up what looked like the worst sort of embarrassing swimming costume. 'Mum loves her SealSuit!'

Leonora gasped. She stared at him in total astonishment.

'What the – yes, that's a **SealSuit**, but how could you know that?'

'It's the latest craze if you wanna go really fast in the pool!'

Leonora suddenly felt dazed. The world seemed to slip sideways.

'I – I just don't understand. How could you know about my inventions? Something really weird is going on.'

'I'm not joking. They're everywhere.'

'There must be a logical explanation – I just can't see it.' Leonora jumped up and started pacing the room. It was several minutes before she paused, rubbing her forehead with her wrist.

'Of course, there's one place I might find some answers.'

'Where's that?'

'Uncle Luther's study. If he is who you say,

there might be some evidence in there. But it's always locked and he could come creeping back *any minute*! It's like he has anti-fun radar for catching me out. So we'll have to be quick!'

Jack gulped. Twitchy squarked. Leonora's stomach flipped. She knew they had to break into her uncle's study right away. And – *almost impossibly* – they had to avoid getting caught.

# 7
# Uncle Luther's Study

'Hey, Leonora, wait up!' cried Jack. Leonora was sliding down the banister at high speed, as if riding a gigantic helter-skelter. She jumped off at the second floor, landing in front of a room with a thick steel door. It was covered in bleeping scanners, combination locks and a sign saying **GET LOST!**

'This is it?' she heard Jack blurt out, as he and Twitchy arrived panting behind her.

'Yes, it is.' Leonora tried to ignore the fear sloshing around inside her. Uncle Luther could be back at any moment. What would happen if he found out about Jack? Or discovered them trying to break into his precious study? It was the most dangerous thing she'd ever attempted. Even worse than that one time she'd tried to fly a knitted jetpack.

'We're going to need dynamite or something,' said Jack, nodding at all the locks. Twitchy flattened his ears and hissed at the door, then retreated behind Leonora's legs.

'Hey, it's OK, I can fix this,' Leonora said, pulling a mysterious black disc from her tool belt.

'What's that?'

'It's my **X-LOX**. Uses some serious maths to crack any door code in the world.' Leonora set about examining every inch of the door. Then she clamped the **X-LOX** on to its surface using bendy cables. After what seemed like an eternity of clicking dials, tapping in numbers

and muttering, Leonora finally shouted, 'Ha, that's it – I've got it!'

There was a flash of orange light. A noise like distant thunder. The mighty door slid open. Leonora and Jack exchanged nervous glances, then stepped over the unwelcome mat and into the room.

It was cold and sparse inside. There was a wardrobe, a bed and a desk. In one corner was a tower of encyclopaedias so dry and dusty even the bookworms had given them a miss. And across the desk Leonora noticed scattered pieces of something. It was a wooden model of the human heart. She couldn't decide if it had been dissected on purpose or smashed to bits in anger. There wasn't time to ponder.

'We've got to be fast – make sure everything's left the way we found it.' Jack nodded in agreement and they set to work. But it wasn't long before they'd exhausted every hiding place.

'It's no use. I thought I'd find some of my designs or documents – or *something*,' Leonora groaned.

'No, wait – what's he found?' Twitchy was scrabbling his sharp claws on the bed. Jack stuck his arm underneath the mattress and pulled out a photo album. He handed it to Leonora. Inside there were no family pictures, just a gold invitation with swirling black writing. It read:

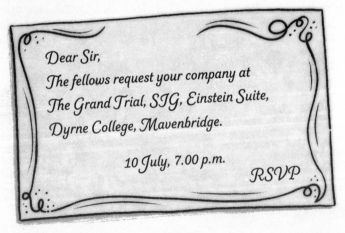

Dear Sir,
The fellows request your company at
The Grand Trial, SIG, Einstein Suite,
Dyrne College, Mavenbridge.

10 July, 7.00 p.m.

RSVP

'What do you reckon that means?' said Jack.

'I – I've no idea. Looks like some kind of test, but I've never heard of SIG . . . and that date – it's in three days.'

'Hang on, something's fallen out.' Jack handed her a newspaper clipping that had fluttered from the album to the floor.

# THE DAILY SNOOP:
## Top Boffins Lost in Polar Puzzle

The scientific community was left stunned today by news of the mysterious disappearance of leading academics Eliza and Harry Bolt. The couple had been travelling on a research boat, HMS *Invisible*, to conduct experiments in the Arctic Circle. An extensive search found no trace of the missing pair. They leave behind one daughter, Leonora Bolt, aged three years.

Leonora felt a great jab to her insides. Words swam before her eyes – 'Top Boffins' – 'leading academics'.

'Leo, are you OK?' said Jack.

'I – I don't understand.'

'What is it?'

'It says here my parents were lost on some kind of *expedition*. That they were top scientists. I thought they were *shopkeepers*.'

Jack frowned. Twitchy nuzzled his head against her legs.

'Something's wrong. I mean, I don't really remember Mum or Dad even though I miss them . . . so much. Wish they hadn't left me with *him*. But I didn't know they were in the Arctic!' Leonora kissed the faded picture. 'I – I need to find out what really happened to them.' She stashed it, along with the invite, in her top dungaree pocket, next to her heart.

'Come on,' she said at last, scooping Twitchy

into her arms, 'let's get out of here and find Millie, before my uncle comes back and catches us!'

'Will Millie be able to help?'

'Probably not. She doesn't usually know what day it is. But she might be my only hope.'

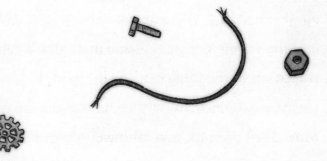

# 8
# Eliza and Harry Bolt

'Oooh, you buttercups hungry again so soon?' Mildred cried, as Leonora, Jack and Twitchy burst back into the kitchen. She wiped green entrails down her apron and hefted a broken teapot on to the table.

'No, we're definitely not hungry. Millie, we've just found something out, something really *strange*.'

'Hmmm, what'll that be, me little sugar-plums?'

'Jack thinks he knows Uncle Luther. On the mainland he's a – a celebrity or something.'

'A celebrity?' Mildred gave a nervous chuckle. 'Well, I don't rightly knows anything about that.' She quickly turned away to stir a cauldron on the stove.

'It's true,' said Jack. 'He's really famous. And we just searched his creepy room and found this invitation to a trial thing.'

'You – you went into his *room*?' Mildred gasped and spun round.

'We *had* to, Millie. And we found this –' Leonora held out the newspaper clipping – 'it's about Mum and Dad!'

Mildred took the invitation and newspaper clipping and read them with a strange expression on her face. When she looked up, Leonora noticed that, for once, Mildred's eyes weren't dancing about as if they'd been invited to separate discos. They were staring straight at her. And they were filled with something she'd never seen before. Fear.

'OK, Leo,' Mildred said softly. 'I suppose you've found out a few things . . . I knew the game was up as soon as Jack arrived. I thinks it's time I told you what I know. You'd better sit down.' Her voice had dropped an octave and she was shaking. Leonora and Jack sat at the table.

'So, the thing is . . . I means, the truth is –'

'Yes?' said Leonora, anticipation bursting inside her.

'There's something I've hads to keep secret all these years . . .'

'What?' said Jack.

'Well, I should tell you –' they held their breath and leaned forward – 'the truth is . . . the truth is that I am an ingenious genius!'

Silence.

The words, once launched into the air, seemed to hover as convincingly as tiny flying pigs. Leonora didn't know what to say. Jack swallowed a fit of giggles.

'O-Kaaaay. Well, that's – brilliant news!' Leonora said, getting up to leave.

'Leo – I knows what you're thinking: old Millie's just gone mad –'

'Not just,' muttered Jack.

'Please – let me explain.' Leonora saw the worry on Mildred's face. She sat back down.

'It's a long story. But I used to be . . . well, I was a professor. A lady fellow at the Society of Ingenious Geniuses.'

'So *that's* what SIG stands for,' Leonora said, swapping astonished looks with Jack.

'Yes, SIG. It's a highly secret organization filled with the world's cleverest people. I specialized in superfood science.'

'You – you worked as a top *food* scientist?' Now Leonora fought the urge to giggle.

'It's true. I pioneered research into bionic lettuce. Created the world's only auto-regenerating spaghetti. My PhD was all about the medicinal properties of hot buttered toast.'

Leonora checked the kitchen calendar. Was it April Fool's Day? She'd known Mildred for as long as she could remember. And if she was an undercover genius, then Leonora was the Tooth Fairy. But it wasn't like Millie to lie or do anything to hurt her . . . was it? Leonora's head was pounding. Nothing was making sense.

'OK,' she said at last. 'You were a professor

or a genius or whatever – but how did you end up here with me? And what about Mum and Dad?'

'I don't know everything . . . not exactly. You see, your mum and dad were students at SIG too. Harry Bolt and Eliza Brightspark. Young they were, and so clever and handsome.'

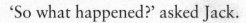

'So what happened?' asked Jack.

'Luther, well . . . he always envied his little sister. Thought his parents loved her more – their golden girl. She got into SIG on a scholarship, so he wanted to get in too. Became *obsessed* with it.'

'But Uncle Luther *is* clever. He's an important professor. Why wouldn't they let him in?' Leonora's forehead creased into a deep frown.

'Not clever enough, for all his showing off. Never could pass the society's trial . . . though it looks like that might have changed.' Mildred laid the golden invitation on the table. They all stared at it. Leonora felt her stomach start to churn.

'What's so amazing about this society?' said Jack.

'It's the most important place of learning in the world,' Mildred whispered. 'The fellows create all sorts of incredible inventions!'

'OK – but what about my parents?' Leonora insisted.

'I was one of your mother's tutors. Shared the job with her favourite teacher, Professor Echo.'

Leonora tensed. *Professor Echo?* That name had a familiar ring. She could have sworn she'd heard her uncle muttering complaints about him once before. But Mildred was hurrying on.

'One day Eliza came to my office and confided something was wrong – thought her brother was *spying* on her. She made me swear to take care of you if anything ever happened to her. Then soon after they – they just disappeared!' Mildred let out a great bellow like a sad sea lion.

'What happened to them? Surely you must know *something*,' Leonora cried.

'I suspected Luther had a hand in it, so I followed him . . . went deep undercover as a housekeeper and we cames here. I thought if you knew the truth you'd try to leave – escape somehow. And then he'd lock you up for good! I've wanted to tell you for so long. Can you ever forgive me, sweetheart?'

Leonora couldn't speak. Her mind was a jumble of questions and broken thoughts. She hugged Mildred as warmly as ever, but the weighty secret seemed to lodge itself between them.

'Millie, I understand you – you were just trying to protect me,' Leonora said at long last, trying to keep her voice even. 'But I – I can't stay here any longer. Everything has changed. I've got to get to the mainland and maybe find SIG – search for clues about Mum and Dad!'

'And I'll help you, sweetheart,' said Mildred, drying her eyes. 'But we must be careful. You get to the beach, see if there are any boats or planes out looking for Jack. And I'll distract Luther if he returns. He mustn't suspect I've told you anything. He's such a dangerous man!'

'Yeah, let's get going,' agreed Jack. 'Won't the ferry be sailing? Or don't you own a boat or something?'

A boat? Leonora realized that on any other island, it would be a perfectly sensible question. There would be boatloads of boats. They'd be knee-deep in dinghies, awash with yachts. But Uncle Luther had taken the only speedboat. And the ferry was hit and miss, quite literally. They'd need another plan.

# **Chapter 8** *and a Teeny Bit*

WE INTERRUPT THIS CHAPTER TO BRING YOU THE
CRABLINK FERRY TIMETABLE FOR THE NEXT 150 YEARS:

JANUARY - no ferry service available. We'd
like to apologize for any inconvenience caused.
But we're really not going to.

FEBRUARY - see January.

MARCH - out to lunch.

APRIL - hourly service sailing.
(Just kidding, YOU MASSIVE APRIL FOOL!)

**MAY** - be ferries, maybe not.

**JUNE** - ferry service will run on days without a letter 'Y' in them.

**JULY** - ooh look! Juggling badgers!

**AUGUST** - why are you still reading this?

**SEPTEMBER** - leaves on the sea, ferry services are TOTALLY CANCELLED FOREVER AND EVER AMEN. THE END.

**OCTOBER** - bah!

**NOVEMBER** - get a bus. or a dinghy. Or a pogo stick. We honestly don't care.

**DECEMBER** - these mince pies really are delicious.

# 9

# Kaaaaaaaping!

Down on the jetty, Leonora stared at the endless blue horizon through her **bionic telescope**. The horizon stared back without blinking. Nothing came into view except bully seagulls trying to do splats on Twitchy. There was no sign of Uncle Luther's speedboat, so they were safe for now.

But frustration flooded through Leonora like the rising tide. It seemed that everything she knew about her life was a lie. Millie was a genius? Could it be possible? How could she have kept it a secret all these years? And what did Uncle Luther know about her parents disappearing? Leonora swore she wouldn't stop for a single second until she uncovered the truth.

'You sure you can trust her?' said Jack. 'Mildred, I mean?'

'Millie's always looked after me,' she replied, uneasily.

'Then how come she never helped you get out of here? It's weird, don't you think?' There was a long silence. The sea breeze chilled their skin. Leonora tried to ignore the weeds of doubt busily sprouting in her mind.

'I'm not sure,' she said, finally. 'Just hope that I can get us out of here.'

Leonora took a deep breath and tried to focus on possible escape inventions. Could they use the **MoleStar ocean bed tunnelling machine**? Too slow. Or those **day-glow**, **extendable sea stilts**? Too dangerous and/or ridiculous. Then there was the **Switcheroo** – could that work? Maybe.

But she'd had problems with the prototype overheating. And the real machine wasn't quite finished yet . . .

'I reckon we wait it out. Dad and my big brother, Jim – they'll rescue us in our dinghy. Or the Snorebury lifeboats will arrive soon.'

'Lifeboats?' Leonora narrowed her eyes. 'You think they'll be looking for you?'

'My family – the whole village – will be out! My mum will be going nuts. And I'm playing in the football cup final next week, so they'd better hurry up!'

Leonora felt a twinge of envy. She wondered what it would be like to have so many people worried about you, out searching for you.

'You know Crabby Island isn't easy to find, don't you? We'll need to help them.' She crouched down and rummaged in her rucksack, pulling out a catapult, a box of matches and what looked like several metallic

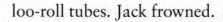

loo-roll tubes. Jack frowned.

'Homemade **rainbow flares**. Been dying to try these out.'

Leonora picked everything back up and jumped down on to the beach. Jack followed behind with Twitchy, who was letting out a series of long-suffering squarks.

'Hey, what's up, Twitch?' she said, distractedly.

'Not a *total* mystery,' said Jack, eyeing the loud explosives. (Do NOT try this at home. Your parents won't just go completely bananas. They'll go the full fruit salad!)

As Twitchy hid behind Jack's legs, Leonora stared at the horizon. Her mind sketched a series of equations, shapes and angles on to the sky. After a few minutes of muttering about 'projectiles' and 'trajectories', she lit a flare, placed it in the catapult and *kaaaaaaapinged* it out to sea where it exploded. They watched clouds of multicoloured smoke drift away like a unicorn's burp.

'Whoa, that was epic!' cried Jack. 'Let's have a go!' Leonora grinned and handed him the catapult. As the hours slipped by and afternoon turned to evening, they kept sending flares into the sky. Of course, Leonora knew it was probably hopeless. She just didn't want to disappoint Jack with the knowledge that Crabby Island was like the Bermuda Triangle (or the infamous Thai Hexagon). Impossible to leave.

She was just preparing to relay this bad news, when something unexpected caught her eye. Twinkling lights suddenly appeared in the distance –

'It's – it's a BOAT!' cried Jack.

*Was it her uncle? Had he seen the flares?* Her heart pounded against her ribs. No – no – this was a little boat bobbing round the headland towards them. She lifted Twitchy up, and she and Jack plunged up to their waists in the icy waters of the bay. This was it! This was it! They were saved!

But when Leonora realized who the boat belonged to her stomach performed a gymnast's somersault complete with wobbly landing. It was Captain Spang's Crablink Ferry, *Unsinkable 16*.

'Leonora! Wee lass! I saw the flares – you need a lift?'

The ferry pulled up alongside them and, without waiting for an answer, Captain Spang leaned over and grasped Leonora's arm. She felt herself being lifted out of the water, flopping into the boat with Twitchy like freshly caught salmon.

'And who's this wee fella?' Captain Spang asked, fishing Jack out of the water too.

'Captain, meet Jack,' said Leonora, getting unsteadily to her feet.

'Och, good to meet you, young man.

Welcome aboard.' Captain Spang gave them a
neat bow. He was a short, wiry man with a mane
of grey hair and a beard to match. He wore
a billowing white shirt and a red silk cravat.
'You kiddlywinks crossing alone today?'

'Yes – it's just us. Any chance you can get us
to Port Splendid this time? Without the sinking
bit?'

'Och, that last trip was bad luck, terrible

sailing conditions,' he said, with a casual shrug. 'And the time before we only got a bit wet. No harm done, eh? Now, make yourselves comfortable.'

They sat down in the shabby boat, wet clothes squelching.

'Well, that was easy to catch a lift,' said Jack, as Captain Spang started the engines.

Leonora nodded, trying to ignore the butterflies multiplying in her stomach. Was this the day she'd leave her home – finally see the mainland? Could they sail away to safety at last?

But then the butterflies started full-on partying. Because instead of doing any actual sailing, Captain Spang sat down beside them and pulled out a battered guitar. He coughed nervously, thumbed the strings and began singing. He had a glorious voice, like buttered honey, deep and rich and full of powerful emotion. Shame about the song though, that was rubbish:

*I've sailed across the oceans blue,*
*And seas of green, I've sailed them too,*
*Black Sea, Yellow Sea, the one that's red,*
*I've even sailed the sea that's dead (Dead Sea),*
*But I'm always sailing back to you,*
*Your heart is pure, your love is truueee!*

'Don't we need someone to steer?' interrupted Jack. He nudged Leonora and tried to send her a message through the medium of GIGANTIC EYES. By now a storm was brewing. The sky was as black as a bat's pyjamas, and furious clouds were trying to pick a fight with each other.

'Och, don't worry,' chuckled Captain Spang, 'these modern boats pretty much sail themselves. Would you like another song? I used to sing with the Peruvian Ladies' Nose Flute Quartet. Kinda tricky listening but some interesting harmonies.'

'Um, OK – great,' she mumbled. Jack gave

her a dig in the ribs.

'Sit back and relax. I'll have you on the mainland before you can say "easy-peasy"!'

But after several more hours of sailing, nothing was looking easy (or peasy for that matter). Captain Spang had finally stopped singing. He was behind the wheel, desperately trying to steer the stricken boat.

Wind howled; rain lashed their faces. There was the most incredible **KERASH!** And then a **SMAAAAACKLE!** The *Unsinkable 16* had run aground.

'Is this it? Port Splendid?' cried Jack. 'Ooof! What's that *smell*?'

Leonora knew the apocalyptic stench could only mean one thing – they had sailed in a circle – crashing right back on to Crabby Island! And worse than that – much worse than everything – it was the Cave of Tremendously Terrible Terror!

# 10

# The Cave of Tremendously Terrible Terror

'Shall I reverse?' cried the Captain, as violent waves shoved the ferry even further up the black beach.

'No, we've got to get out – take shelter in the caves!' cried Leonora.

'Well, I'm not going in there! Every sailor knows about that Frark beastie!'

'Come on,' cried Leonora, 'or we'll all be washed out to sea!' She tucked a wriggling Twitchy under her arm and leaped with a **SHOOOSH** into the wet sand. Jack followed behind with the Captain, who was clutching his beloved guitar. They stumbled up the fast-disappearing beach towards the caves. Then it hit them. *The stench.*

It was like nothing on earth. Imagine putting a dead mackerel in your granddad's sock. Then leaving it on a warm radiator for a week or twenty. Then taking the sock, rolling it in old cowpats and adding it to a sack filled with unwashed pants. The smell was something like that only much, much (much, much) worse.

Leonora fumbled in her pockets and pulled out a torch. It only gave a weak halo of light but at the cave's mouth they could finally see the source of the pong. On a table sat a quadruple portion of

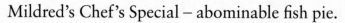

Mildred's Chef's Special – abominable fish pie.

'Oh, thank goodness it's just that!' cried Leonora, picking up the plate at arm's length. She carried it out on to the beach and chucked it into the ocean, which appeared to retch and shudder.

'It dinnae look that bad, just needed a wee bit of ketchup,' said the Captain.

'Yes, but what's it doing *here*?' said Leonora, as she rejoined them. 'Someone's trying to put us off the scent!'

'Well, they succeeded – I think my nose is actually dead!' said Jack. Then he turned and whispered, 'Leo, it's all so obvious: Mildred put it here. She must be working with your uncle!'

Leonora stared at Jack. Her throat tightened. 'No – no that can't be true. There must be another explanation. Come on, we've got to find out what my uncle is hiding!'

More determined than ever to solve the

mystery, Leonora led them out of the storm and into the dank cave. It took a few moments for their eyes to adjust to the gloom. And then they witnessed something that made their jaws drop on the floor, their eyes pop out on stalks and their hair stand on end. All in that order. It was a mountain of treasure so stupendous that it reached up as high as the stalactites (which always hold on tight).

There was a solid gold chimpanzee guarding suitcases stuffed with rubies. Stardust tiaras illuminated the cave walls, which were hung with paintings of the *Mona Lisa* and the *Cheerful Lisa*. An antique violin played by Count Alexander Sparkle Fingers himself lay next to a signed copy of the *Complete Works of Shakespeare*. There were even Fabergé eggs and spoons, and a Rolls Royce carved from Italian marble.

'This has your uncle written all over it!' cried Jack. Sure enough, every bit of treasure was labelled 'Property of Lord Luther Brightspark – So Get Your Sticky Mitts Off!'

'So, the Frark legend was a trick – a trick to hide all this treasure!' Leonora cried. 'My uncle really has been making money out of my inventions. Can't believe I never suspected. I'm so stupid!'

'No, Leo, don't say that!' urged Jack. 'Your uncle knows exactly how clever you are – that's how he made all this – *loot*.'

'Your uncle did this?' said Captain Spang, eyeing the hoard. 'What sorta uncle is he?'

'The worst sort,' Leonora groaned.

'I know rich people hide their money but this is *ridiculous*. You cannae let him get away with it!'

'Yeah, we need to get out of here, fast,' agreed Jack. 'If your uncle finds out we know his secret, he'll never let you leave. He'll never let any of us leave!'

'No, he won't. Come on then – hurry – to the boat!' cried Leonora.

They turned from the treasure hoard and stumbled back to the mouth of the cave. But Leonora realized the ferry was too far away to reach. The ocean suddenly belched and surged, lifting the little vessel and sending it crashing sideways. *Unsinkable 16* was smashed into a bazillion matchsticks before their eyes.

They were trapped.

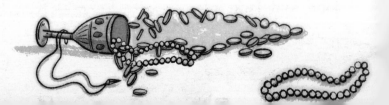

# 11
# Caving-in

That night seemed as long as a month of Mondays. The storm raged outside the cave. The Captain raged inside the cave.

'Another boat – gone!' he cried. 'That's sixteen in a row. I just dinna ken how it keeps happening! Whatever will I tell ma boss at Crablink?'

'D'you think maybe it's time for another job?' said Jack, who was standing up to his waist in great mounds of treasure (he was sporting a fur coat, a glittery gold chain and the lost crown of Liechtenstein).

'Aye, maybe it's time for a change, time to hang up ma Crablink hat,' he sighed. 'I'm getting too old for this . . . but I've always been a sailor, you know? Whatever else will I do? What do you think, Miss Leonora?'

Leonora didn't respond. She was slumped in the shadows, hugging Twitchy to her chest. Her uncle had lied about everything. Her whole life. They were *poor*, he'd told her. And all the while he'd been living in luxury. Stealing her inventions. Had he stolen her parents too? And what did *Mildred* know about it all?

Tears filled her eyes but she shook them away. Her ideas were good. They were *really* good. A super-massive-mountain-of-treasure good. A spark of determination ignited inside her. She would fix this, escape the island and discover the truth once and for all!

'There must be a way out of here – *here* – *here*!' Her voice echoed in the darkness as she sprang to her feet.

'Yeah, there must be. I'll help you look,' said Jack, looking eager to escape the serenading that was about to start. While Captain Spang tuned his guitar and launched into a soulful rendition of 'I Lost My Boat in Timbuktu', Leonora, Twitchy and Jack searched deeper inside the caves.

The torch flickered feebly in the darkness. Water cascaded from above. Everything felt slick and slimy to the touch. Leonora realized that Twitchy had disappeared ahead behind a jagged wall of rock and was squarking at something. They squeezed through a narrow gap to join him. There, hidden behind a pile of dried seaweed, was a wooden door.

'This is it – our way out of here. Well done, Twitch!' Leonora said, crouching down to look at the door. By now, Captain Spang had finally stopped warbling and come to help them. He pushed his slender shoulder against the door but it wouldn't budge.

'Och, it's jammed tight.'

'Couldn't you use the **X-Lox** again?' suggested Jack.

'No, it won't work on this. The door's sturdy and made of high-density oak, so we'll need explosives or tunnelling equipment, or –'

'Or . . .' Jack flashed his lopsided smile and disappeared. Several minutes later he returned, panting and dragging a hefty diamond and ebony sceptre. 'Or we could just bash it to bits with this?'

'Och, easy-peasy!' cried Captain Spang.

Leonora nodded. 'Diamonds are really hard

so they should help weaken the timber. I'll try first.'

Using all her strength, she lifted the sceptre like a baseball bat and hammered it into the door. Over and over she bashed. With every strike she thought about the lies that her uncle had told her. And the names he'd called her. *Stupid. Little. Mess.* A new and ferocious energy coursed through her veins. The door didn't stand a chance.

'Leo, stop – you've done it,' said Jack.

The door hung aside and through splintered wood they could just make out a staircase built into the rock. It looped upwards into inky blackness. 'Come on,' she said, dropping the sceptre and catching her breath, 'let's just get out of here.'

One by one they clambered through the doorway and up the stairs. Around and around they trudged, higher and higher, until they eventually came to another unlocked door. Leonora realized at once where it led. It was the perfect hiding place for a secret staircase. Somewhere no one in their right mind would go: Mildred's appalling pantry.

'Oh, I've been worried sick! Thank goodness you're safe!' cried Mildred, as they all trooped through the pantry and out of the kitchen back door, gasping great lungsful of fresh morning air. Mildred hauled herself off a stool to greet them.

'The boat was smashed up – we found treasure in the caves – a secret staircase!' cried Leonora, the words cascading out of her.

'Oh sweetheart, I knew about that old staircase! I did not know it led down to them caves though,' said Mildred. 'Luther's work again.'

*Just Luther's work?* Leonora felt doubt gnawing at her.

'Is he back?' said Jack, eyeing Mildred suspiciously.

'No sign of him yet. Been up all night keeping watch.'

'Why, Miss Mildred,' said Captain Spang, stepping forward, 'always such a – a pleasure to see you!' He removed his cap and gave her an extravagant little bow.

'You daft old fool! You could have been killed!' Mildred cried. She put her hand on her hips and glared at him.

'Aye, those were awful conditions,' he said,

sheepishly, 'but I'm retiring – honest I am! You were right. Sea's no place for a man my age.'

Mildred gave an exasperated snort, although Leonora noticed a look of fondness pass between them.

'Come on inside then, I've gots mussel muesli for breakfast. Maybe you can explain how we'll get away from here without your boat.'

Mildred turned to go inside. And Leonora was about to follow when she felt Twitchy's whiskers brushing against her leg. Somewhere in the distance they could hear something – a hypnotic thrum – the sound of chopper blades! A shiny speck was flying low over the sea towards them, closing fast. They watched it getting closer and closer until eventually it was near enough for them to see the pilot. Leonora's heart pounded – her insides lurched.

Uncle Luther was back!

# 12
# The Golden Helicopter

Black clouds ambushed the sun and bundled it away. A huge golden helicopter was now buzzing in the sky right above them like a glitzy wasp. There was no time to run and hide.

Uncle Luther waved at them from his seat in the cockpit. Then nudged the joystick sideways and landed expertly on the clifftop right beside the lighthouse.

'Uncle Luther!' Leonora blurted out, as he swung open the helicopter door and climbed down. He was utterly transformed. His brown corduroy suit – gone! His bald head gone!

He had thick dark hair, tanned orange skin and teeth as white as snowdrops.

'Leonora, my darling niece!' he cried, waving a silver cane in their direction.

'B—but what are you *wearing?*' she said, stumbling backwards as her uncle strode from the helicopter. Mildred, Jack, Captain Spang and Twitchy flanked her. Uncle Luther stopped in his tracks.

'Ah yes, I saw you had a few unscheduled visitors while I was away. I'm sure they've let the cat out of the bag by now. There's no discipline around here –' he stared at Mildred – 'so no need for that dull corduroy disguise any more. Thought I'd wear my usual attire.'

'What do you mean, *saw?*' Leonora said.

'Didn't I mention? I've been watching you closely all this time. Couldn't have you trying to make a run for it. Wave at the birdies!'

'Y—you've been *spying* on me?'

'Well, spying is an awfully strong word. Let's say keeping tabs. Terribly useful, these flying informers.'

Leonora looked up and noticed for the first time that some of the gulls were wearing something – little white collars! The perfect place to hide cameras.

Her insides twisted. So *that's* how he knew her every move. He'd been spying on her, just like he'd spied on her mother. Millie was telling the truth!

'You – you're nothing but a liar!' she shouted.

'A liar? My dear, what's all this nonsense?'

'You *stole* my ideas!'

'I merely . . . *borrowed* them.'

'We found out your secret! There's no Frank – just mountains of treasure!'

'Gosh, you really do have a vivid imagination.' He sighed, leaning on his cane.

'All this time I've been stuck here and you –

you were living in luxury! And my parents –'
Leonora took a bold step forward – 'what
happened to them? They didn't just *disappear*!'

'What do you know about that?'

'I know about the Arctic. I know they
shouldn't have been out there – they would
never have left me alone!'

'Ah yes, your mummy and daddy –' Uncle
Luther gave a dramatic pause and smoothed
down his greasy wig – 'went off seeking
academic glory and abandoned you. So, make
no mistake – *you're mine*.'

Leonora shrank back. Her head was
spinning. 'They were coming back for me! I
know they were. But you – you stopped them!'

'Did I? My little sister, the *golden girl* –' his
words dripped with spite – 'and her oh-so clever
husband. Not my fault they went on an Arctic
jaunt and got themselves . . . *lost*.'

'Bet it was,' said Jack.

107

Uncle Luther grimaced. 'Ah yes, the castaway. Homesick yet? Another few weeks of Mildred's hideous fish food and you'll be throwing yourself back in the sea.'

'Leave him alone!' Leonora clenched her fists. 'You can't keep us here – we're *all* leaving, right now!'

'Go on then. Off you pop. Borrow the chopper if you like. But leave now and you'll never know the *truth*.'

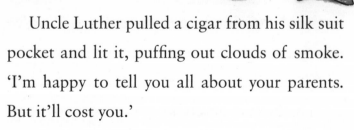

Uncle Luther pulled a cigar from his silk suit pocket and lit it, puffing out clouds of smoke. 'I'm happy to tell you all about your parents. But it'll cost you.'

'Cost me what?'

'I'm not asking for much –' his mouth curled into a nasty smile – 'I simply want . . . I need you to finish the **Switcheroo**!'

'I – I don't know what you're talking about,' Leonora said, willing her voice to sound steady as her stomach dropped. She realized her secret was out.

'Oh, I think you do. This Friday I've been invited to the Society of Ingenious Geniuses to present my best work to the fellows. If I pass the grand trial, I'll finally take my rightful place amongst their esteemed ranks. And then . . . my *real* work can begin.' His eyes suddenly glimmered with the dreamlike shine of a  maniac. Beads of sweat trickled down his forehead. He crumbled the lit cigar to pieces in his fist.

'What work can begin – what do you *mean*?'

'The fellows have all kinds of secrets that I can put to good use . . . like Insignia's emotion formula . . .' He suddenly stopped. Leonora thought she saw something strange. Something she'd never, ever seen before. An intense feeling seemed to flash across her uncle's face. He looked . . . *lost*. But a moment later it was gone.

'And what if I don't agree to this – this *deal*?'

'Well then,' he said, snapping back into the moment. 'You'll never be free. And you'll never know the truth about your parents.'

Leonora's heart thrummed. She couldn't let him have the **Switcheroo** – it was her most powerful invention. But she also realized that Uncle Luther had the thing she wanted – needed – most. He held the key to the missing part of herself. The part that had disappeared with her parents.

'OK. You can have it, on condition you fly us out of here,' Leonora said at last. 'And I'll need to finish it.' Twitchy growled. Mildred gave her a desperate look.

'You can't!' whispered Jack.

'I – I don't have a choice.'

Uncle Luther looked flushed with triumph. 'Excellent! I'll give you three hours. And then we'll fly off together as agreed. The clock is ticking, Leonora Bolt.'

# 13
# The Unluckiest Chapter of All

Back upstairs in the workshop, the atmosphere was as tense as ten thousand maths tests. Leonora was hunched over her workbench, adjusting the components inside the Switcheroo.

'So all this time you – you knew he had a double life?' she asked Mildred, setting down her tools.

'I'm afraid so, sweetheart.'

'And you couldn't have got us away?'

Mildred shook her head. 'It was far too dangerous. Luther was always watching. If we tried to escape and failed, I knew he'd take your beloved island away too. He'd keep you locked up inside a dark laboratory somewhere! Least this way you had *some* freedom.'

Mildred bustled over and wrapped her arms round Leonora.

'So we've *both* been prisoners?'

'It's never beens a hardship for me,' Mildred whispered, her eyes shining with tears.

In that moment, Leonora felt a whole galaxy of understanding pass between them. Mildred had protected her, made her island a home. Given her the space to dream and to grow. And Mildred had surrendered her *own* freedom all these years. How could Leonora ever have doubted her? They stayed hugging each other for a long while.

At last Jack coughed, interrupting them awkwardly –

'Um, Leo, time's running out.'

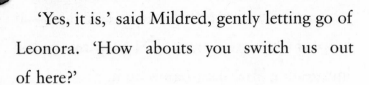

'Yes, it is,' said Mildred, gently letting go of Leonora. 'How abouts you switch us out of here?'

Leonora sighed. 'If we do that, I'll never know about my parents.'

She picked her tools back up and carefully finished fixing circuit chips printed on to layers of silicon. Then she checked the power supply to the quantum processors one last time, before sealing the casing together. At last it was . . . *finished*.

But a queasy feeling was rising inside her. Could they be about to leave Crabby Island? She suddenly realized why it had taken her so long to build the Switcheroo. She didn't want to leave the only home she'd ever known. The world beyond seemed vast and terrifying. She stared at the machine as if it was cursed.

'I've gots a bad feeling about all of this,' said Mildred, echoing her thoughts. 'He's after

Insignia's *emotion* formula, whatever that is. If he passes the trial, there'll be nothing to stop him getting his greedy hands on it!'

'Emotion formula?' Leonora frowned. Whatever would her uncle want with emotions? Could he somehow steal those too? Bottle them, sell them? Or worse . . . *control* them? She remembered the smashed wooden heart on his desk. Her blood froze.

'You're right; it's all a really bad idea. We can't let him anywhere near SIG or that formula!' Leonora rubbed her forehead and took a deep breath. And as she let it out, she felt the gears in her mind clunk into action.

'What if – what if I don't give him the real Switcheroo at all? What if I give him the prototype?' She strode over to her desk and pulled out the hidden box. Inside was the slightly smaller but otherwise identical contraption.

115

'If I remove the prototype's memory module, it won't work. So . . . Jack and I could meet Uncle Luther and demonstrate the real Switcheroo and get him to tell me about my parents. Then we'll create a diversion and swap it for this broken one. He'll never know the difference until he's flown us to the mainland!'

'That's a great plan, sweetheart,' said Mildred.

'Aye, should be easy-peasy,' agreed Captain Spang.

Jack frowned. 'Can't we just wait for my dad and the lifeboats? I'm *sure* they'll be here – any minute now.'

'I don't think they will,' said Leonora, gently. 'We'll have to fix this mess and get out of here by ourselves.' Jack's face fell; he turned pale.

'Yeah, s'pose you're right,' he said eventually. 'No one's coming. Maybe . . . I can help you with the diversion bit.' He gave Leonora a determined look. She nodded back. For the next few minutes, they planned the deception. Then Leonora gathered her things and they headed for the bedroom hatch.

Outside, the scorching sun made beads of sweat drool down their spines. Everything felt shimmering and unreal as they walked down towards Libra Beach, watching Uncle Luther getting closer. They finally stepped out on to the hot sand only a few metres away from him.

'You're late,' he hissed. 'Have you brought it?'

'Yes. But first I want your word. I give you the Switcheroo and you – you'll tell me what happened in the Arctic. Then fly us out of here.'

'Yes, yes –' he shot her an irritated look – 'now let me have it.'

Leonora pulled the rucksack from her back and crouched down, carefully removing the Switcheroo and lifting it for her uncle to see.

'What in heaven's name is that?' he snapped. 'It looks like a hairdryer!'

'How would *you* know?' said Jack, eyeing Uncle Luther's ludicrous wig. 'Why do you even want it, anyway? Isn't a cave full of treasure enough for you?'

Uncle Luther glowered at Jack. But he seemed strangely pleased with the question.

'Oh, money and fame are wonderful, of course. But one does tire of them. There's only so much endless champagne and sports cars and palaces a man can tolerate. I want the real prize. I want Insignia's formula . . . to harness its energy, understand how it feels to . . .'

There it was again! A look of torment flickered in her uncle's eyes. He coughed and quickly regained his self-control –

'This contraption of yours will help me pass

their trial. Now, I suggest you give me what I want!'

He stepped forward and towered above her, watching her every move. Leonora felt sick. With trembling fingers, she tried to conceal that she was entering coordinates into the machine. Then she fumbled around for a stick and a rock. Pointing the nozzle at the stick she tapped in more numbers. There was a whirring noise and a burst of invisible energy. The two objects vanished – then reappeared in the opposite places!

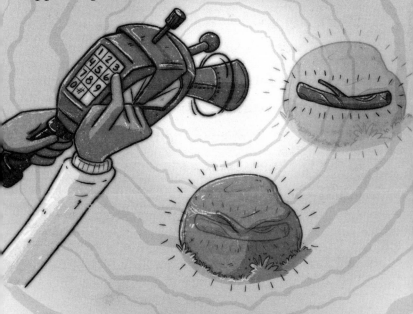

Uncle Luther and Jack gasped in astonishment. Leonora repeated the process, swapping the two objects back again.

'Whoa, that was epic!' cried Jack, his eyes alight with wonder.

'Told you – nothing's impossible,' said Leonora. 'I mixed quantum mechanics with nanocomputing and bits of a recycled fridge and – ta dah!' *Not a stupid little mess any more*, she thought.

'How marvellous!' cried Uncle Luther. 'I always knew being strict would spur you on to greater things. Seems I was right again! Now, hand it over.'

Leonora hesitated. She glanced behind her uncle to the clifftop. Mildred, Captain Spang and Twitchy were guarding the helicopter next to the lighthouse. *Stick with the plan.* She sniffed loudly, which was Jack's signal to –

'Oh, it's so hot I – I feel weird!' he cried,

tumbling forward on to the sand. Leonora gasped and rushed to help. She crouched over him, making a great fuss and secretly exchanging the machine for the prototype tucked inside his waistband.

'What the – stop fooling about!' cried Uncle Luther. Jack lay doubled over, moaning, while Leonora stood up again. Her pulse was thrumming. She handed her uncle the prototype.

'Oh, this is good, this is very, very good.' His eyes shone with demented joy.

'Now – our deal. What happened in the Arctic?'

'Hmmm?'

'Tell me about my parents!'

Uncle Luther sneered. 'I can tell you that they are –'

'Yes?'

'They're . . .'

'What? Tell me!'

'Your parents are . . . *alive*.'

'Alive?' Leonora felt her heart leap. *Alive – alive – alive!* The word circled like a merry-go-round. Could it really be true? She scanned her uncle's face but for once he looked like he was telling the truth.

'B—but where are they? Please – you have to tell me!'

At that moment, a seagull swooped down. It pecked furiously at Jack's head.

'Ow, get off!' he yelled, jumping up and batting the gull away. Leonora's insides lurched. The real **Switcheroo** was revealed in the sand where Jack had been lying.

'Oh, Leonora. You weren't trying to *trick* me?' said Uncle Luther. He bent down and grabbed the real machine, tossing her back the prototype. With a nasty smirk, he aimed it directly at his loyal seagull.

'I think I just saw how you did this,' he said, keying in coordinates and targeting the helicopter in the distance.

# THROOOOOOOSH!

There was a whirring noise and a colossal and invisible burst of energy pulsed through

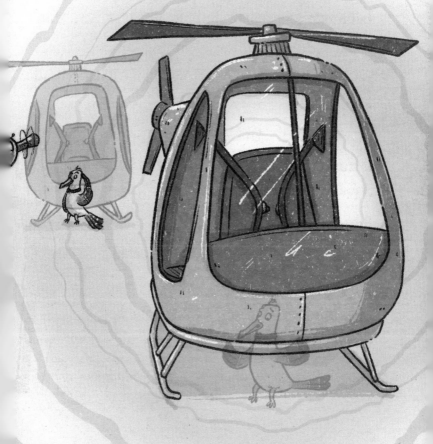

the atmosphere around them. The air rushed past at immense speed, flexing and forcing its way outwards. Everyone was knocked to the ground. Then, just as suddenly, the wind dropped again. The air returned to normal as if nothing unusual had happened. As if the boundaries of physics hadn't just been stretched like bubble gum. When they finally looked up, the gleaming helicopter was parked on the beach before them. The seagull had vanished.

'Splendid!' Uncle Luther shrieked. Before Leonora or Jack knew what was happening, he dashed towards the helicopter and jumped in. The engines roared to life and it lifted up, up and away into the dazzling blue sky. Leonora and Jack were left choking in the sand.

## 14
# Easy-peasy Plans

'Nooooo – he's getting away!' cried Leonora. She sprinted across the beach, hot sand bursting behind her heels. Up the cliff path she ran. Jack raced after her. When they finally reached the lighthouse, their faces were slick with sweat and they were panting like Labrador puppies.

'Whatever happened?' cried Mildred.

'The diversion didn't work! He's got the real Switcheroo. But he told me something down on the beach,' she cried.

'He told me that my parents – they're still alive!'

'Alive?' Mildred gasped. Her eyes filled with tears. 'Little Eliza? Me darling Harry? Oh, Leonora!'

'Lass, that's wonderful news!' cried Captain Spang.

'Yes, but he didn't tell me where they are – they could be anywhere!'

'Leo, you'll find them,' said Jack. 'If you can make something as cool as that machine, you can do anything!'

Leonora blinked and rubbed her forehead. She knew that Jack was right. She'd created a machine that was . . . *incredible*. But Uncle Luther had stolen it. Their best means of escape – years in the making – gone! Then she suddenly noticed something else. The seagull that had been Switcherooed was lying beside them where the helicopter had been. And it was now just a pile of smoking feathers.

'Oh, this is no good – no good at all!' Leonora cried. Panic gripped her like a vice. The Switcheroo, her machine, was *dangerous*. And she'd just unleashed it on the world. Her uncle would pass the trial, get into SIG and steal the formula! There was no way to stop him.

'This is all my fault. I didn't think it through enough. And now we're stuck, he's – he's taken everything!'

Leonora felt a sudden tidal wave of helplessness wash over her. She sank to her knees and buried her face in her hands, letting out gasping sobs. Her shoulders rolled and heaved. He was always one step ahead of her. Too clever, too powerful. *She could never win.*

'Please don't give up, sweetheart. If anyone can fix all this, it's you,' whispered Mildred.

'Yeah, we're in this together – we're a *team*,' said Jack. 'Let us help!'

'Aye, we're at your service,' said Captain

Spang. Twitchy thudded his tail in agreement.

Leonora looked up at them. Her eyes flicked from Mildred to Jack, to Twitchy and Captain Spang. All of them were on her side. All of them were willing her to succeed. She blinked tears away. Her uncle hadn't taken everything from her at all. He'd left the most important, most valuable things behind.

Leonora picked herself up and the five of them pressed together in a big hug. She made a silent vow. She'd dismantle the mountains, drain the oceans, she'd unscrew the entire universe piece by piece to stop her uncle – and find her mum and dad.

'OK, you're right,' she said, as they parted at last. 'We can do this . . . but it looks like easy-peasy won't cut it. We'll need something bigger, bolder, something . . . *audacious*.' Leonora picked up a stick. Her plan sprang to life in the dust.

'We're going to make a balloon using the lift basket and any washed-up bits of the ferry. Jack, I'll need you to trawl the beaches for fishing lines, vines – anything we can make into ropes.'

'No problem,' said Jack, firmly. 'I've got this.'

'Millie, we're going to need lots of inflatable things. And some sort of gas to make them float.'

Mildred looked thoughtful. 'We've got beach balls, shower caps – some old space hoppers. Leave the gas to me.' Jack stifled a snigger.

'And Twitch' – Leonora bent down, rubbed her nose against his – 'I'm going to need you to distract the spy gulls. Keep them over on the south side of the island. We can't let Luther know we're following him!'

Twitchy's little eyes stared up at her. Then to Leonora's surprise, he stopped his usual trembling and rose up on his hind legs. He scanned the skies, gave her a determined squark and hopped off towards Lynx Lagoon. She felt her chest squeeze.

'Och, if I may also be of assistance –' Captain Spang coughed, then pulled a scroll from his frilly sleeve – 'wouldn't be much of a sailor without a map!'

'Not much of a sailor *with* one,' muttered Jack. Leonora elbowed him and thanked the

Captain. Then she uncurled the scroll for them to read.

'The rainforests of Sweden? The Welsh barrier reef?' said Jack, frowning.

'Och, no, not that one.' Captain Spang chuckled. He rummaged in his other sleeve. 'Here – try this.'

Leonora surveyed the second map. It was just as she'd calculated. The mainland was about 70 kilometres away.

'Right, we're going to fly over to the mainland and find Mavenbridge *here* . . . I think.' Leonora frowned. Geography wasn't her strong point. Her uncle had ensured there were no maps on the island. 'Then we're going to find Dyrne College *here* and break into it. Even though it's probably the most fortified building in the world.'

'You're right about that – guards everywhere,' said Mildred.

'Then we'll find the Einstein Suite and stop the trial. All in –' she checked her watch – 'two days.'

'Och, you missed the bit about wrestling the Switcheroo off your uncle,' said Captain Spang. 'We'll need to do that too!'

'Yeah, of course we will. Otherwise it would all be far too simple!' Leonora's face flushed with a kind of manic delight. The plan was, quite simply, insane. But they had to be bold, be daring. Now was the time to think big – think beyond her little world.

'Right, then,' she said, pulling a screwdriver from her tool belt. 'Let's get to work!'

# 15
# Up and Awaaaaaaargh!!!

Early the next morning, they were all tucked inside the wicker basket on top of Orion Heights. Above their heads bobbed hundreds of freshly inflated household items, including bin bags, birthday balloons, washing-up gloves and Jack's lobster. They were filled with gas from a batch of Mildred's lethal fermented caviar (**Gruesometer** scale: Red).

'Right, is everyone ready?' said Leonora. They all exchanged terrified glances. Leonora felt like her insides were trying to find an emergency exit. Would the basket take their weight? Would it even fly? Or would they all be smooshed to bits on the rocks below? She shook the thoughts away and set her expression to 'relaxed and confident'.

'OK, Captain, on my signal, let's go!' Leonora chopped her arm through the air. Captain Spang untied the ropes and they lifted a few centimetres off the ground. The wicker creaked. The inflatables jostled like horses at the start of a race.

Jack had turned the worst shade of queasy-green. Mildred clasped a frilly handkerchief to her face. Only Twitchy, who was pooped (and pooped on) from spy-gull distraction, looked calm for once. Nothing happened for a few, tense minutes. But then the breeze picked up and slowly, unsteadily, downright wonkily, the balloon/zeppelin/flying-lobster/thingamy carried them up, up and up a bit more into the glorious summer sky.

Leonora watched her home, her old life, slipping far away until it became a speck in the distance. Her throat felt choked. She wondered if she would ever see her precious island again. Ever run free along its grassy dunes and swim in its crystal waters. She forced the painful feelings away. At long last, this was it – this was her moment. The day was alive with the most wonderful possibilities. The *world* was alive with possibilities.

But after several long hours in the creaky basket, the possibilities weren't looking quite so alive. They were looking distinctly unwell and like they might need putting to bed early. The basket dawdled a couple of metres above the green ocean. An elderly sloth in concrete flip flops could have outrun them.

'We need to be lighter – reach the higher atmosphere, the faster winds,' said Leonora, scanning the cloudless sky. 'Must have something in here to help.' She picked up her rucksack and as she rifled through it, a series of equations and aerodynamic designs seemed to scroll before her eyes.

'Millie,' she said at last, 'did you bring any sundresses?'

'Course . . . not quite your size though, sweetheart.'

'Doesn't matter. I think we can make this basket really fly!'

'How?' said Jack. 'There's no wind – we're stuck.'

'Here, take these and start cutting them into long strips.' Leonora handed Jack nail scissors and half a dozen of Mildred's vast nylon frocks from her suitcase.

'Och, if I may be of assistance,' said Captain Spang, 'I'm pretty handy with a needle and thread. Used to be head costumier and lead guitarist for the Lithuanian Rebel Operatic Ensemble.'

Leonora blinked. 'O-Kaaaay. Well then, you can do the stitching.' She handed him the sewing kit and he gave her a delighted grin. Over the next few hours, Leonora and Jack cut up strips of fabric. Captain Spang and Mildred deftly sewed them back together again. As the light started fading, they'd finally finished what looked like a huge flowery sack.

Mildred bashed open a tin of caviar and struck a match. **HISSSSSS!** Fishy gas ignited and started burning. She carefully angled the tin so that its warm vapours filled the sack, which slowly got bigger and bigger. It rose up out of the bottom of the basket to join the inflatable things above, glowing like a grandma's lampshade in the darkening sky.

'We did it!' cried Leonora, as the basket started to climb.

'Whoa, we so did!' agreed Jack.

'Aye, we're really flying now,' said Captain

Spang. The basket rose higher and higher. Soon they were sailing at terrific speed.

'Uh, just checking . . . how will we stop?' said Jack.

'Don't worry, it'll be totally fine,' said Leonora. 'When we reach Mavenbridge I'll do a controlled landing – set us down quietly in a field outside the city.'

It was now pitch dark, and Leonora couldn't see the panicked expression on Jack's face. And she was too distracted anyway. There in the distance she could just make out white cliffs and – yes – the mainland!

They sped ever onwards. Leonora's eyes flooded with tears. A huge lump lodged itself in her throat.

After all these years, she'd done it!

Soon they were flying

high over land. An immense black patchwork stretched out far below them. It was studded with blinking lights, moving this way and that. Leonora thought it looked like the most magnificent electric circuit board.

'Oh wow,' she whispered. 'It's *amazing*!'

Mildred squeezed her shoulder. 'I always wanted to show you this, sweetheart. This big, beautiful world of ours.'

They flew on in silence. Leonora hardly

dared to blink in case she missed anything. And they were making good time. Mavenbridge was now only 81.52 kilometres away. Leonora checked the wind speed using her homemade paper-cup **anemometer**. She estimated the journey should take four hours and thirty-three minutes. Then all they had to do was find Dyrne College and stop the demonstration tomorrow night. Everything was going to plan – exactly according to plan!

Until they totally crashed.

## 16
# Mavenbridge

They landed with a colossal **THWUMP**.
Not into a field, as Leonora had been
hoping, but into the side of a building.
Lady Snumpington-Falcon's eighteenth-century
ornamental clock tower. It was the pride of
Mavenbridge's Heritage Department and was,
up until that moment, a priceless city centre
landmark.

'That what you call a controlled landing?'
groaned Jack.

'Ooooof, sorry, couldn't slow down. Is
everyone OK?' Leonora had been distracted
by the sheer excitement of her new

surroundings. They'd drifted wildly off course – narrowly avoiding six electricity pylons, two petrol stations and a field full of irritable goats. Unfortunately, they hadn't avoided the clock tower's rococo dial, bits of which were now decorating their hair and clothes.

'Aye, we're OK,' said Captain Spang, patting what he thought was Mildred's hand but was actually Jack's face. Twitchy gave a mournful *squark*. Mildred was wedged sideways, her feet in the air. It was all far from dignified.

'Let me see if I can work out where we are,' Leonora said. She scrabbled around for her torch and shone it upwards. The balloon's fabric was wrapped around the tower's weathervane. They were suspended high above the cobbled city streets. In fact, the only thing that stood between them and certain pavement-death was Captain Spang's remarkable stitching.

'Right, let's keep really still. Maybe I can drop ropes over the side for us to climb down.' As she said this, the balloon fabric ripped and the basket plummeted downwards another few metres. It swung from side to side, like a giant pendulum.

'Um, maybe not,' said Jack.

It was a long, uncomfortable night. None of them dared move a muscle. As dawn finally broke, the city was slowly bathed in gold and lilac light. Leonora gazed out over Mavenbridge as if in a trance. Burnished rooftops, towering church spires, the wide, shimmering river. It was all so *beautiful*.

'Leo, I think we've been spotted,' said Jack.

'Hmmm?'

'Look down.'

She snapped out of her daze and noticed a handful of people had gathered below them, apparently in charge of pointing and gawping at the stricken basket. By nine o'clock, the pointers had been joined by a dozen head-scratchers. By eleven o'clock there were policemen, paramedics, shopkeepers, tourists and even a local film crew all swarming about.

By one o'clock, firemen had at last succeeded in rescuing them. (It had taken several attempts to cajole a reluctant Mildred down the spindly ladders braced against the side of the tower.) When they were all finally safe on the ground, a wall of faces stared at them. Leonora had never seen so many people – so many cross people – in one place before. It would be her uncle's idea of a cocktail party.

A reporter thrust a microphone into Mildred's face. 'So, how does it feel to have destroyed one of the city's most loved and valuable monuments?'

'I . . . er, what's that?' said Mildred.

'Thirty years of painstaking restoration

ripped apart in one night. Care to comment?' sneered another reporter. An angry murmur elbowed its way through the crowd.

'I don't knows anything about that!' Mildred said, wringing her hands.

'It was me! I broke it, but it was an *accident!*' cried Leonora. All the snappy faces turned towards her instead. She felt a wave of embarrassment hit her. She hadn't expected her first contact with the outside world to be so . . . *hostile*. She wanted the ground to swallow her up. Or preferably swallow *them* up. All four hundred of them.

Eventually, a policeman pushed along to

the front of the crowd and shooed the reporters away like flies. He smoothed down his thick moustache and started asking them a whole new set of questions.

'That your basket, Miss?' he asked, nodding towards the tower.

'Yes . . .'

'You know you can't park it there?'

'I didn't. I mean I was trying to, you know, not *die*.'

The policeman glared at them, puffed out his chest. 'I should take you all down the station!'

'You cannae do that,' cried Captain Spang. 'We're the victims of an accident!'

'Oh, yes, I can! For flying without due care and attention, defacing a public monument, ownership of a dangerous wild animal.' He scowled at Twitchy, who was trying to disappear behind Jack's legs.

*This is it,* Leonora thought. Her first taste

of freedom and they were going to be arrested. Right here and now. But as the policeman was about to escort them to a waiting van, Captain Spang pulled out his guitar and stepped forward. He gave Leonora a knowing wink and strummed a few chords.

'Och, if I may, ladies and gentlemen, not often I get to perform in front of such a large – such a *wonderful* crowd,' he said, leaning into a reporter's microphone. 'I'd like to play you a few songs from ma travels. These come from the Himalayan Pensioners Amateur

Yodelling Collective – feel free to sing along with the chorus!'

With that, Captain Spang launched into a song. But this was no soppy love ballad. It was far more dangerous. He started making a warbling sound so high-pitched that, at first, the whole crowd was mesmerized, as if staring into the eyes of a snake.

'**AIOOOOOOOIAAAAAA-IOUUUOIAAAAOUUUUU!**'

As the song continued, people began to gasp and cover their ears. Captain Spang's

throaty vibrations and grunting grew louder. Dogs started howling. Shop windows shattered. Everyone was suddenly hurrying to get away. Mothers grabbed their children and bundled them into buggies. Burly firemen fled the scene, sobbing hysterically.

'Quickly – now's our chance!' whispered Leonora. She grabbed Twitchy and started backing away. Jack linked arms with Mildred and they shuffled backwards too. Slowly they edged further from the crowd. Then they turned on their heels and ran.

'Calm down! Stop it – we need order!' cried the hapless policeman, as people shoved past him. In the chaos, no one had seen the adventurers slip away.

They hurried down narrow streets and onwards into the heart of the city. When they finally paused beneath a grand stone archway to rest, Leonora was relieved to see

Captain Spang appear.

'Did you see that – the crowd – they loved me!' he cried, hugging his guitar to his chest.

'They did?' said Jack.

'Aye, just wanted to create a wee diversion. Wasn't expecting them to scream with excitement like that! Always thought I could be a lead singer. Just a shame they all had to leave so quickly. Guess it's lunchtime or something, eh?'

'Yep, something like that,' said Leonora, grinning with disbelief. 'How did you lose that policeman?'

'I exited stage left when he was busy trying to calm my new fans. First rule of show business – always leave 'em wanting more. He might catch up with us though . . .'

'Yes, we should get going . . . but well done, Angus,' Mildred said gently. He blushed to the tips of his ears.

'You daft old fool. Now, we've got to find Dyrne. It's right over on the eastern side of the city. Might take a while with my old knees. We'd best get going!'

They set off again, this time with Mildred leading the way. But their progress was slow. Mildred kept having to pause in the shade to rub her swollen legs, and they lost their way more than once.

Down twisted alleyways they stumbled, past ancient buildings with turrets and towers. There were courtyards and fountains and statues of scholars in fancy robes. The whole city looked to Leonora like it had been designed by a highly enthusiastic but delirious elf. She'd never dreamed of such

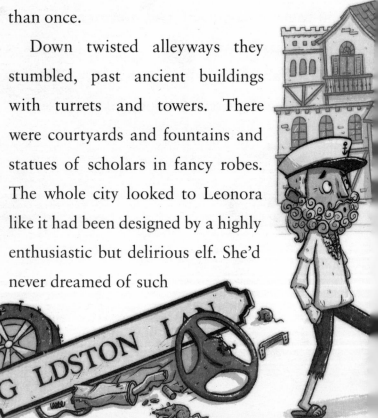

an incredible place. It took her breath away!

When they finally reached Goldstone Lane, however, she got her breath right back. Was this really the home of SIG? The most advanced scientific headquarters in the universe?

There must have been some mistake.

# 17

# The Hidden Plaice

'Millie, you *sure* this is right?'

They had stopped in front of a dilapidated row of old buildings. Rusty shopping trolleys and rubbish were strewn all around. Rats scuttled in the shadows. The only sign of life was a grim little chip shop. The Hidden Plaice.

'This is it,' Mildred whispered in a reverential tone.

'No, it can't be – we must have taken a wrong turn!' Leonora stared in disbelief. But, sure enough, a sign at the end of the street, just visible behind a burnt-out car, read:

G LDSTON LAN

'Oh heavens,' Mildred muttered, patting herself down, 'I'm underdressed!'

Leonora glanced at their outfits and frowned. She didn't know much about fashion but was sure their dragged-through-a-hedge-backwards look pretty much suited the surroundings.

'Millie, we don't have time to change! We don't have time for anything!' The city bells suddenly started chiming in the distance. It was now five o'clock. Only two hours until the trial – two hours to stop her uncle!

Mildred smoothed down her vast sundress, then led them along the litter-strewn lane and through the chip shop door.

It took a few moments for their eyes to adjust to the dark. The tiny shop stank of rank cooking fat. Greasy wallpaper peeled limply from the walls. Mildred rang the counter bell, which gave a feeble tinkle.

'Millie, what are we doing here? It can't be right,' Leonora said impatiently. Every atom in her body was tense. And the clock on the wall seemed to be speeding up time – 5.15 – 5.20 – 5.25! She noticed that Twitchy's whiskers, in fact his whole body, was vibrating.

But just at that moment, there was a rustling sound and a nervous-looking woman appeared behind the counter. Leonora realized that, whoever she was, she didn't spend her days dishing up cod and chips. Beneath the oil-splattered apron, the woman wore an expensive black suit. She had neat red nails and a long brown plait that swung down her back.

They stared at each other. No one said a word. Then the woman covered her cheeks with her hands –

'Professor Dribble!' she cried. 'Can it – can it really be you?'

'Professor Puri!' Mildred gasped.

The woman rushed from behind the counter
and wrapped her arms tightly round Mildred's
considerable middle. Tears were streaming
down her cheeks.

'Oh, Mildred, I always *dreamed* you'd come
back!'

At last they parted and stood with hands
clasped together, beaming at each other. Then
Professor Puri hurried to the door, locked it

and pulled down tatty blinds.

'You must excuse me,' she whispered. 'We simply can't be too careful.'

'Careful about what?' Leonora whispered back.

'Security. This is a highly classified location.'

'It is?' said Jack, gazing longingly at the fried onion rings.

'Yes,' she repeated. '*Highly* classified.'

'Please, we're not here to cause any trouble,' Leonora said. 'We just need to get inside Dyrne College, right away!'

Professor Puri narrowed her eyes. 'That information is strictly confidential,' she said, 'until I know to whom I am speaking. Professor Dribble, who is this young lady?'

Mildred pulled Leonora to her side. 'Professor Prisha Puri, meet Leonora Bolt. Eliza and Harry's little un!'

Professor Puri took in a sharp breath. Then

her lips curled into a smile. 'Dearest little Leo, so grown up! My goodness me, don't you look like your mother!'

'You know my mum? And my dad too? Do you know where they are?'

The professor flinched, then shook her head. She motioned for them all to sit down.

'First, you need to tell me what has happened to you. I need to know everything.'

So, while Jack helped everyone to triple portions of chips and mushy peas, Leonora poured out the story of her life as quickly as she could. Crabby Island, her terrible uncle, Mildred's undercover disguise, the Switcheroo – the fact that her parents were still alive, *somewhere*.

'We've got to stop my uncle. He's trying to pass the SIG trial. He wants to become a fellow and steal Professor Insignia's emotion formula. He'll only use it to – to control people, to make them miserable. We can't let him anywhere near it!'

Professor Puri listened without interrupting. Her face was impossible to read. Then she let out a long sigh and said, 'As Professor Dribble knows, I'm a research scientist at the Society of Ingenious Geniuses. We operate from our top-secret headquarters in Dyrne College.'

'So, it *is* here?' Leonora frowned.

'Yes, you've come to the right place. We're hidden in plain sight. No one would guess that this very building houses the most sophisticated research and technology facility in the world.'

Leonora eyed the stained yellow tablecloths, the mouldy ketchup bottles, the wonky plastic chairs. 'I guess not,' she agreed.

'I can take you to Dyrne College and smuggle you into the Einstein Suite . . . but it won't be easy.' Professor Puri pressed her fingertips to her temples, as if trying to soothe a headache. 'I've always suspected he was crooked, but Lord Luther's vastly wealthy, with powerful friends. He'd stop at nothing to have such a formula, use it for his own, dark purposes. But . . . it's your word against his.'

'There never was a man less true to his word,' said Captain Spang.

'Be that as it may, how are you going to stop him?' asked the professor. 'If this Switcheroo machine is as powerful as you say, it sounds supremely hazardous. I cannot allow you to endanger yourselves.'

Leonora felt suddenly dizzy. Up until this moment, she'd only been focusing on getting to Mavenbridge and finding Dyrne. Now the insane danger of her mission was dawning on her. Uncle Luther could turn the Switcheroo on her. She could end up like that seagull.

'Professor Puri,' she said, trying to sound confident, 'this is how we're going to stop Uncle Luther.' She fumbled in her rucksack. 'This is the first Switcheroo I made, the prototype. I can use it to stop the trial if I'm in the same room. I know it won't be easy, but we need to be . . . *daring*.'

Leonora handed over the machine to Professor Puri. Then she patted her top pocket. The memory module she'd removed earlier was inside.

'Very well,' Professor Puri said at last. 'I will take you to the Einstein Suite. But I can only take one of you. It's heavily guarded. The fellows will start gathering soon.'

'She cannae go alone!' cried Captain Spang. 'That man – there's no telling what he'll do!'

'Yeah, let me go too,' pleaded Jack. 'We're a team!'

'No, Jack,' said Leonora. 'You need to get

home safely – your family will be sick with worry. And I . . . I have to face him on my own.'

Twitchy let out a gigantic **SQUEEEAAAARNOMP!** (which roughly translated means 'take me too!'). He rose up on to his hind legs, glaring at her with ferocious affection. She buried her nose in his fur. 'You've been brave enough, Twitch. I'll be right back, I promise.'

There was just enough time to say goodbye to Mildred. 'I love you, Millie,' she whispered.

'Oh, Leo, I love you too, sweetheart. We won't let him win.' They stood holding on to each other as if clinging to a life raft. Then Leonora reluctantly let go.

'Quickly, there's no time to delay,' said Professor Puri. Leonora nodded and picked up her rucksack. She managed one last flimsy smile. Then she followed the professor past the shop counter, through a curtain and down into darkness.

## 18

# A Half-eaten Jar
# of Peanut Butter

Leonora followed Professor Puri down a long
flight of stairs, trying not to topple over in the
pitch black. Her heart thumped. There was a
bitter tang in her mouth. After several minutes
of silent descent, they stopped.

'I'm going to pretend you're supplies from
the chip shop,' said the professor, guiding
Leonora to step into a cramped cardboard box.
'Please – this is very important – don't make a
single sound!'

Leonora squashed herself into the box and
Professor Puri closed the lid. Pins and needles

stabbed her limbs. There was a flash of light. The sound of a heavy door clunking shut. Leonora felt the box being tipped backwards on to a trolley. They were on the move! After what seemed like a month but must have only been a few minutes, the trolley stopped.

'Quickly – quickly – get out,' said Professor Puri, opening the box.

Leonora squinted as her pupils were flooded with yellow evening light. It looked like she'd been smuggled into a high-tech palace. They were in a grand corridor with vaulted stone ceilings and stained-glass windows. Instead of oil paintings, flat-screen computer monitors covered in lines of code hung on the corridor walls. Professor Puri pulled her behind a nearby velvet curtain.

'I have taken you as far as I can,' she whispered. 'This is Dyrne College. The room you want is the second door to the right. The

trial will be starting – make haste!'

The professor hugged her briefly, then disappeared back behind the curtain. Leonora peeked out, watching as she walked down the corridor and approached a burly security man. He was standing only a few feet from the door Leonora needed to take, his back turned. The door was open with only a velvet rope across it. A conversation started. This was her chance!

Leonora slipped out from behind the curtain and crept along the right side of the corridor. She edged closer and closer, keeping low to the ground with her body pressed against the wooden panels. Through one of the windows opposite she could see into a courtyard where Uncle Luther's golden helicopter was parked. Her blood ran cold.

Then, suddenly, Professor Puri's voice was raised in anger. The guard sounded flustered. While he was still facing the other way,

168

Leonora sprinted forward, ducked under the rope and into the Einstein Suite.

The room was stifling and dark. At the far end a lectern stood on a bronze stage. An elderly gentleman with a freckled brown face was on the stage, addressing the audience. Leonora counted – there were just thirteen other people. *So, these are the fellows*, she thought.

Leonora crawled along the floor at the very back of the room and hid in the shadows. Fumbling in her rucksack she pulled out the prototype Switcheroo, then looked back to the stage. The man was concluding his speech.

'And so, without further ado, my fellow fellows, I must welcome a true innovator – Lord Luther Brightspark!'

There was a polite ripple of applause. Leonora's body thrummed with fear. On to the stage – only a few feet away – strode Uncle

Luther. He smiled at the audience, flashing those expensive teeth, and took the microphone from its stand.

'Honorary fellows, I must thank Professor Insignia for that splendid welcome. Tonight, I hope to show you a machine of such power and magnificence that I may prove my worthiness and become . . . the fifteenth fellow!'

*Over my dead body,* Leonora thought, before wishing she hadn't chosen those particular words. There was another murmur of applause. Leonora peeked out over the seats as far as she dared.

'Now, brace yourselves for a night of wonder! You're about to witness an unrivalled advancement in human technology!' Uncle Luther gestured towards a wooden box sitting on a small table to his left. *The* **Switcheroo** *must be in there*, Leonora thought. This was her moment.

Leonora reinserted the memory module into the prototype. Then she tapped numbers into the keypad. But there was no whirring noise – no blue light. It still wasn't working!

'I think it's fair to say that none of you will  be prepared for the true brilliance of my latest invention . . .' Uncle Luther was now strutting up and down the stage like a peacock. Leonora felt as if the room was spinning round her, faster and faster and out of control. She tried every combination of codes, but her prototype was just a lump of dead metal. *Silly. Little. Mess!*

As the words taunted her, she took a deep breath and focused like never before. And then she remembered. This machine had problems with its cooling system. Its superconductors wouldn't work in the hot room.

Quickly, she slid open the metal casing. Using a pair of tiny tweezers, she set about adjusting its internal fan, fixing the blades so they rotated at twenty-five times their normal speed. Then she clicked the device back together and tried again. It finally spluttered to life!

'Is there someone there – someone at the back?' said Uncle Luther, squinting into the bright stage lights. Leonora froze. She hardly dared to breathe. But by some miracle her uncle ignored the noise and carried on. 'No? Well, let's not waste any more time. I present to you, the one – the *only* – **Switcheroo**!'

Uncle Luther lifted the lid of the box just as Leonora finally managed to programme the correct codes into her machine. A blue triangle of light radiated out. She lifted her head above the seat, pointed the prototype at the box on stage and **FROOOOOOSH!**

An invisible pulse of energy tore through the room like a sudden tornado. It rushed past the audience at incredible speed, forcing them all back in their seats. Uncle Luther's oily wig was whipped clean off his head. Then just as quickly the tornado stopped. The room returned to normal. The audience all jumped up. Leonora could hear angry voices.

'Dear fellows, my apologies,' said Uncle Luther, holding up his hands. 'That's all part of the demonstration!' He gave a strained laugh, sweat pouring from his brow.

Leonora looked inside her rucksack. It had worked! She'd done it! The switch was complete. She now had both of her incredible machines. She felt overjoyed. When her uncle found out what she'd switched his for, he wasn't going to be happy. It was definitely time to leave.

But then Leonora hesitated. She might have two Switcheroos but Uncle Luther still had one important thing she'd come for. How could she leave without knowing about her mum and dad?

Worry immobilized her body. Doubt crowded

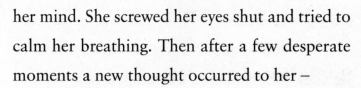

her mind. She screwed her eyes shut and tried to calm her breathing. Then after a few desperate moments a new thought occurred to her –

The helicopter.

*Of course.* Uncle Luther must have flown to Dyrne from somewhere. Could he have come from seeing her parents? Could there be clues in the cockpit? She realized that she'd never get another chance like this. She had to try and get inside!

Leonora crawled back towards the door. Outside, the security guard was still being told off by Professor Puri –

'No, young man, I wouldn't trust you to guard my goldfish!' Her voice rose to a shrill crescendo as she glimpsed Leonora sneaking behind them once more. Leonora gave her a quick thumbs-up, and tiptoed towards the helicopter in the nearby courtyard. Uncle Luther, meanwhile, was coming to the end of his presentation.

'Once more I give you my greatest work – the **Switcheroo**!' He flipped open the wooden box and with a theatrical flourish pulled out . . . a half-eaten jar of peanut butter!

Silence.

'No, no there's some mistake – it can't be. My machine!' Uncle Luther cried, looking aghast at

the empty box. There was a snigger from the audience. Then another and another.

'You don't understand – someone must have taken it!'

'Switched it?' muttered an impatient voice.

'Total waste of our time,' said another.

'He's as nutty as that peanut butter,' heckled a third.

That set the rest of the audience off. The fellows started roaring with laughter, cheering and clapping with mock enthusiasm.

'That was your last chance, Luther!' hissed Professor Insignia, as he jumped up and swept past the stage. 'I won't put my neck on the line for you again! You're nothing but a cheap showman. A disgrace!'

With that, he and the other professors hurried out of the lecture suite. Luther was left alone under the hot stage lights, his face a twisted mask of fury and despair.

# 19

# The Old Library

Leonora crouched down on white leather seats in the helicopter cockpit, trying hard to stop trembling. The satnav on the dashboard winked at her, displaying nothing but a bewildering series of maps and numbers. Now she understood why her uncle had never taught her geography. None of it made sense.

She jabbed at the screen with her fingers, trying to find details of the helicopter's last journey. Outside she heard furious muttering, followed by the crisp tap of cane on stone. With one last desperate swipe of the screen a set of coordinates flashed in front of her. But before she could memorize them, the pilot's door flew open. Uncle Luther's bloodshot eyes met hers.

'I knew it was you!' he screeched, scrambling over the seat and grabbing her by the wrist. For a split second, the force of his fury seemed to weld her to the spot. But Leonora's arms were slick with sweat and she managed to wriggle free. Out of the cockpit she slid. Then she bolted back across the courtyard.

'Quickly – guards – stop that girl!' Uncle Luther raced after her, as angry as a hornet in a hurricane. Leonora sprinted down the nearest hallway, shoes squeaking on the marble floor. She thought for a minute she'd lost him – but no – Uncle Luther was hot on her heels.

This way and that she darted, left and right. Dyrne College was a maze of long corridors and dark laboratories. Soon she was hopelessly lost. Where was the chip shop? Where was Millie? She couldn't slow down. Lungs burning, ears ringing – every fibre in her body was longing to find a way out!

She spun left and fled down another corridor, before realizing too late that there was only one door. She ducked behind it and found herself in an old library. As quickly as she could, she tiptoed across the room and concealed herself behind a bookshelf at the far end. Maybe he hadn't seen her . . .

Her heart capsized. She heard the awful tap-tap-tapping of his cane. Uncle Luther entered the library and slammed the door shut. There was no way out.

*This is it*, she thought. She was trembling all over, dizzy and sick. From her position behind the bookshelf she could just make out Uncle Luther's shiny black shoes. They slowly started walking towards her.

'Dearest Leonora. Whatever have you done?' he said in a sickening voice. She shrank further into the shadows. Fear played her spine like a xylophone.

'I know you're in here. Why don't we talk awhile?'

Leonora let out the breath she'd been holding. She thought of her lost mum and dad. Summoning all her bravery, she stepped out from behind the bookshelf. They stood face to face, only a short distance apart.

'Ah, there you are, you silly little mess!' he hissed. 'Just like you to ruin everything! Ten long years I've been waiting to become a fellow and you – you trashed my chances in one night.

So now I'll make you pay!'

He lunged for her. But Leonora lifted her arms and pointed the **Switcheroo** directly at him. He stopped – stepped backwards – raised his hands.

'Stay where you are!' she shouted.

'Easy now . . .'

'Don't move or I'll –'

'Or you'll *what?*'

'I mean it – y-you just move away from the door – let me go!'

'Let you go? I have no intention of letting you go *anywhere*. You humiliated me!'

'I – I didn't mean to make you look stupid. You did that yourself!'

'That was my big chance. Now all my plans are in tatters! I've waited years – *years* to finally get my hands on Insignia's emotion research . . . you've destroyed everything!'

'They'll never let you into the society now.

The fellows know exactly what sort of man you are – a liar – a fake!'

'You don't understand – I *need* that formula of his!'

His voice was suddenly choked. He ran a shaking hand across his brow. Leonora saw the look of desperation on his face. Despite everything, she couldn't help but feel strangely sorry for him. He looked pathetic – so lost and unhappy.

'It's not too late for you to do what's right!' she cried. 'Let me out of here. Let me be with my mum and dad!'

Uncle Luther let out a long sigh and stared at the floor. His scrawny shoulders dropped. She thought for one fleeting moment that he was about to change his mind – that he was about to let her go. Instead, he looked up and fixed her with his glacial glare.

'Spare me your little sob story. Parents aren't

all they're cracked up to be. Mine weren't. And I won't stop until I have that formula, do you hear me? Human beings . . . they're so *weak*, so easy to manipulate. I will be the first person alive with the knowledge to harvest their emotions!'

*Harvest?* The word made terror flood through Leonora's body.

'Yes, you heard me correctly. And you, my little apprentice – or should I say *accomplice* – will help me!'

'No – there's no way I'm going to help you do that!' she cried.

'Well then, I won't give you what you want. Those coordinates you stole from my helicopter won't help. I have your parents far too well hidden. I'll ensure that you never, ever find them!'

'You won't keep them from me forever!' cried Leonora, the **Switcheroo** wobbling in her outstretched arms.

He loomed over her, his face bright with rage.

Leonora stared up at this broken, twisted man. As much as she longed to find her mum and dad, she wanted to stop him much more. And she had the power to teach him a lesson.

He sprang forward – but she was too fast for him this time. She programmed her machine with coordinates for the place of her childhood nightmares – the Cave of Tremendously Terrible Terror.

Everything happened all at once and in a mesmerizing blur. There was a whirring noise and a triangle of cold blue light beamed from the Switcheroo. She felt an overwhelming rush of relief as it engulfed her awful uncle.

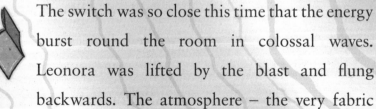

'**ARGHHHHHHH**!!!!' he screeched. The switch was so close this time that the energy burst round the room in colossal waves. Leonora was lifted by the blast and flung backwards. The atmosphere – the very fabric

of time and space – snapped and flexed round them. Books tumbled from shelves. Papers blew up into the air. Windows rattled and smashed. There was an immense, universal roaring noise and then . . . nothing.

Nothing.

Nothing.

Nothing.

Just before Leonora's head hit the library floor – just before she tumbled into black unconsciousness – she could have sworn she saw a solid gold chimpanzee sitting right next to her.

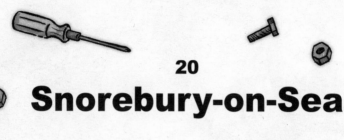

# 20
# Snorebury-on-Sea

'Leonora, Leonora – can you hear me?'

'Owwww!' Leonora awoke with a start. She tried to blink the world into focus. She was in a strange bedroom. Sunlight streamed through the curtains. A heavy scent of antiseptic filled the air. Mildred, Twitchy, Jack and Captain Spang were all waiting beside the bed, their faces etched with worry.

'Me little sugarplum,' Mildred whispered, leaning forward and stroking her hair. 'You had us proper worried and no mistakes.'

'Aye, it's good to have you back, lass,' said Captain Spang.

'Where am I?' Leonora's throat felt like she'd been gargling cement. In fact, her whole body felt as though she'd been run over by a cement lorry.

'You're at a safe house in Snorebury,' said Jack. 'We were brought here undercover by SIG so I could get back to my family while you got better.'

'And you're *alive*,' said Mildred, clasping her hand and raining kisses down on it. Leonora could feel the tickle of tears. Twitchy hopped on to her pillow and licked her face, making everything whiff of sardines.

'Now then, how's the patient?' Professor Puri quietly entered the room with a tray of breakfast.

'All sorts of awful. What happened?'

Professor Puri set the tray down. Then she lifted Leonora's wrist and took her pulse. 'You sustained a bad concussion. But now you're most definitely on the mend. Here, try to eat. As Professor Dribble knows, hot buttered toast has excellent healing properties.'

Mildred and Professor Puri exchanged smiles and helped Leonora sit up. In between mouthfuls of toast, she tried to piece together the last few days. She could just about remember the clock tower crash – Mavenbridge – Goldstone Lane. And then her whole body shuddered. *The library*.

'Wh-what happened to Uncle Luther?'

'We were rather hoping that you could tell us,' said Professor Puri, fixing Leonora with a thoughtful look. 'It appears as if he has completely vanished off the face of the earth.'

'But he was there, in the library, he tried to –'

'Oh, we know what that terrible man tried to do. But the CCTV in Dyrne Library showed him there one moment and then – poof! A golden chimpanzee took his place. Can you imagine such a thing?'

'I think I can,' she said. 'He's back in the caves. Hope he's enjoying all his stolen treasure.'

'Yeah, and Millie's vintage pies,' said Jack, flashing his lopsided grin.

Leonora smiled at Jack. She felt relief and joy waltzing around inside her. Jack had made it home. She'd succeeded in this most important mission. And she'd stopped Uncle Luther. He'd failed the trial thanks to her, lost the emotion formula and had been banished!

But then a dark thought occurred to her. Had he ended up like that seagull?

Then another dark thought.

'He – he didn't tell me where my mum and dad are. I couldn't get the helicopter coordinates. And he said I'll *never* find them!'

Professor Puri seemed to flinch. 'Indeed . . . our forensic experts searched the helicopter. We found the coordinates but I'm afraid it's a mystery. They lead to a location in the middle of the ocean.'

'The ocean? Then that must be where they are!'

'I think that's highly unlikely. Luther was simply covering his tracks. The location is hundreds of miles from land. But take heart. Now we know your parents are alive, we'll do *everything* to help you find them.'

'We'll all be together again one day,' said

Mildred. 'I swear to you!'

Tears bubbled over and streamed down Leonora's cheeks. She knew that there was a piece of her heart that would never be whole until she found her parents. She would fix herself by finding them.

'Millie,' she said at last, 'now we're back on the mainland, don't you want to return to SIG?'

'Oh, sweetheart. While you were sleeping, Prisha and I have hads a grand time catching up about our working days. Feels like a long time ago. I'm too old for all that business now . . . it's time for a new generation to join the society.' Leonora noticed Professor Puri and Mildred share a meaningful look.

'Now, young lady, you must rest,' said Professor Puri, gently herding everyone out of the room. When they were alone, she turned and said, 'You are well hidden here in Snorebury. No one knows anything about your past, or how Jack really made it home. And you must keep your special talents a total secret. Try not to draw any attention to yourself. Lie low . . . *blend in*. Your uncle may come looking for you one day.'

Leonora let out a long, deep sigh. 'Thank you – for everything,' she said.

'No – no thank *you*, Leonora. You brought my dearest friend back to me. You are a girl of prodigious talents. Don't ever forget it. You're an *incredible* inventor.'

As Professor Puri left the room, everything around Leonora suddenly seemed to come alive, as if the volume had been turned up. Happiness burst into her heart like teams of tumbling acrobats. And she felt something new and unusual bubbling up from somewhere buried very deep inside her. *Pride*.

Over the next few days and weeks, Leonora tried her absolute, cross-her-heart, pinky-promise hardest to follow Professor Puri's instructions. She began her new life, her normal life – a life with people in it.

Mildred and Captain Spang got married at St Siobhan's church (the patron saint of tricky spellings). They moved with Leonora into a little cottage on Primrose Lane, a few doors up from Jack. And they had neighbours and a corner shop and yoghurt and newspapers and a paddling pool and mains electricity and chocolate biscuits. Everything was utterly, magnificently, staggeringly new.

Captain Spang launched his career as a singer-songwriter, recording his experimental studio album *That Sinking Feeling*. Mildred rediscovered her culinary paradise, her foodie wonderland, a vast, gastronomic portal of delights (or the local supermarket, as everyone else calls it).

Meanwhile Jack became something of a local hero. He never tired of telling his friends (and massively annoying siblings) of how he'd

battled stormy seas and tussled with tiger sharks to rescue himself from his lobster adventure. He'd even been picked to captain Snorebury Flyers in the football cup final.

And Twitchy also settled into village life. He spent contented hours in the cottage garden on Otter Watch, showing the genteel Snorebury seagulls who was the absolute boss.

As for Leonora . . . well, between you and

me, she wasn't planning on staying in Snorebury for long. She spent every waking moment thinking about her mum and dad. Where were they? What had her uncle done with them? She wondered if they missed her as much as she missed them. Leonora knew one thing for certain. She was going to find them. She was going to get her family back. No matter what.

So, she'd been busy sketching blueprints for an experimental homemade submarine. It was a deep-sea explorer made from bits of repurposed lawnmower and old ice-cream tubs. She'd build it and sail it to investigate those mysterious coordinates in the middle of the ocean. But she had to be careful.

You see, Leonora wasn't sure what had happened to her uncle. Had he survived being Switcherooed? Was he now stranded on Crabby Island? And what twisted plan did he want Professor Insignia's formula for? She wondered if – *when* – he would come creeping back.

It meant Leonora had to keep her wits about her. She had to keep an ear to the ground and one eye on the skies (sometimes at the same time).

She would work undercover. Lie low, blend in – not draw attention to herself.

After all, she was a secret inventor now.